CW00970302

A NOTABLE OMISSION

A JANIE JUKE MYSTERY

ISABELLA MUIR

OUTSET PUBLISHING LTD

Published in Great Britain

By Outset Publishing Ltd

First edition published December 2022

Copyright © Isabella Muir 2022

ISBN 978-1-872889-47-4

Isabella Muir has asserted her right under the Copyright, Designs and Patents Act 1988 to be identified as the author of this work.

All characters in this publication are fictitious and any resemblance to real persons, living or dead, is purely coincidental.

All rights reserved. No part of this publication may be reproduced, stored in a retrieval system, or transmitted, in any form or by any means, without the prior permission in writing of the publisher, nor be otherwise circulated in any form of binding or cover other than that in which it is published and without a similar condition including this condition being imposed on the subsequent purchaser.

www.isabellamuir.com

CONTENTS

Easter 1970. A few weeks after the first conference of the Women's Liberation Movement was held at Oxford University, a group is gathering at Sussex University to discuss equality and women's rights...

CHAPTER 1

IT WAS AN ESCAPE of sorts for both of them. Two friends, leaving their problems behind, heading towards new possibilities.

For Janie there were issues at home, not all of which she chose to share with her friend. For Libby, home life was easy. No one to answer to, no one to try to please. The problem for Libby was that work life was easy too. She needed a challenge to shake herself out of the mundane, and this weekend conference at Sussex University offered possibilities. The trouble was that to get there she had to overcome real fear. The thirty-mile drive to the outskirts of Brighton filled her with dread. A dread that had gripped her since she stepped out of bed that Thursday morning.

Her regular car journey; the short distance from Tamarisk Bay to the newspaper offices in Tidehaven was fine; little more than four or five miles. A journey where she knew every bend of the road, every landmark.

A little over a year ago she had moved from Falmouth, returning to her childhood home, securing a better job, and buying her first car. The decision to return to Tamarisk Bay was the right one, as was the job, but the car? It was needs must. Her editor expected her to be first on the scene of any event that might result in a headline-grabbing article. But she wasn't making this trip as a reporter. She was travelling to Sussex University in her own time.

She could have stayed at home and right now she was wishing she had.

Travelling west from Tamarisk Bay, passing the neighbouring town of Brightport, they continued onto the Marsh Road leading to the outskirts of Eastbourne. The traffic was light, for which Libby was silently grateful. Despite it being the Easter holiday period, it seemed folk were still tucked up in bed, more than likely recovering from the previous day's exertions. With the four-day holiday for businesses, and a two-week school break, Easter presented the first opportunity of the year for people to get away. Each spring seaside resorts along this stretch of coastline woke from their winter sleep to become vibrant, buzzing with crowds. The weather was often cold and damp, nothing warming up much before the end of April into May, but holidaymakers didn't seem to care. They were at the seaside and determined to enjoy it. Even when the worst of the coastal wind blew, they could be found sitting on the seafront, or even on the shingle beach, wrapped up in coats, jumpers, and scarves, munching their way through locally caught fish and freshly fried chips. It was a constant surprise to Libby that even the ice-cream vans did a brisk trade.

An hour into the journey and her hands ached from gripping the steering wheel, while Janie relaxed beside her. They were on the ring road, another fifteen miles or so before they reached the university campus. A Volkswagen Beetle suddenly overtook, cutting in so close to Libby's Mini she had to swerve to avoid a collision, hugging the left-hand side of the road and almost driving onto the verge.

'Idiot,' she shouted. But on a chilly spring day, with the car windows closed, the only person to hear her exclaim was Janie, who had complained several times during the journey.

'You know how much I hate being late. We'll be arriving right in the middle of everything. You say you drive slowly to be considerate, but I'll remind you again it's not considerate when you're always late for everything.'

'Don't blame me for drivers who shouldn't be allowed on the road. Do you want me to kill us both?'

'Libby, you've hardly moved out of third gear. It won't be doing the gear box any good.'

'It's when you rush about that you miss things,' was Libby's response. 'You of all people should appreciate the importance of being observant. Anyway, it's not like we have to worry about grabbing the best seats, we're not going to the cinema.'

'I still don't know why I let you talk me into this.'

'You didn't need much persuading, you wanted to come as much as I did.'

When Libby read the article in The Guardian announcing the first Women's Liberation Conference, she was intrigued. The subject sounded fascinating. What's more, the writing style was sharp, witty; something Libby could easily have penned. The article was by a reporter who got a byline in a daily national broadsheet. By contrast, the best Libby could achieve was the occasional front page lead in the Tidehaven Observer, a weekly local with circulation that barely compared to that of a national newspaper.

She presented the idea to Janie as a fait accompli. 'The Oxford conference was the first of its kind, but they're holding others all over the country,' Libby told her friend. 'There's one this weekend at Sussex University, and you and I are going.'

A few days to make plans, to decide which clothes to pack, to get agreement from her editor that she could have two days off. It's just a weekend break, she told him. If anything came from the event it would be for her to use, as and when she saw an opportunity. Her own project, explored in her own time.

'We're here, finally,' Libby said, ignoring her friend's tutting and sighing.

If her driving was slow and considered, Libby's approach to parking was neither. The university's car park was more than half full, an indication of the popularity of the event. She slid her car into the space beside a Ford Capri, her tyres brushing up against the low kerb. She glanced across at the Capri, admiring its sleek form, the orange bodywork and black roof. A car well suited to the driver who stepped out of it. His chestnut brown, bell-bottomed trousers, Paisley shirt every shade of orange, reminded her of the photos of men's fashion she'd marvelled over in a recent newspaper article. John Stephens was setting the trend for men, alongside Mary Quant's fashions for women. Some said the ideas were 'dangerous', 'breaking the mould', but Libby was all for it.

As she continued to study him, the man turned momentarily to look in Libby's direction, his long fringe falling down across his eyes. Seconds later only his back was in view as he walked away from them towards the main university building.

Once out of the car, she grabbed both cases from the boot.

'Here, take yours. We need to be quick,' Libby said, thrusting the smaller case at Janie.

'Now she decides to hurry.'

'We don't have time to dump the bags. Let's go straight to the lecture hall,' Libby said, ignoring her friend's pointed remark.

Any information they had been able to gather in advance about the weekend conference was sparse. The Oxford conference had several hundred delegates, but from the numbers of cars parked, it looked as though this event would be much smaller. She had written in to book a place for her and Janie and received a reply providing few details. They were to arrive no later than two 'o'clock and make their way to the main university building.

'We'll be met on arrival, I expect,' she told Janie, sounding more hopeful than she felt. Instead, if such a welcome was planned, their late arrival meant it was no longer in evidence.

Falmer House was on the far side of the main car park. The four-storey building, predominantly of brick and glass, blocked what little sunshine there was, casting a heavy shadow over Libby and Janie as they approached. Once inside, silence greeted them, alongside a sequence of arrows to follow. The arrows had been roughly drawn on paper and stuck onto the walls along two corridors and up a flight of stairs. At the foot of the stairs, Libby felt a hand on her arm.

'Can I help?' It was the Ford Capri driver, a heady smell of aftershave emanating from him as he moved. 'I'm John, by the way.'

'I don't think we're supposed to ask for help, are we?' Libby said.

The man appeared nonplussed. 'Your case looks heavy, I'm only offering to carry it to the top of the stairs. It's no big deal. But if you'd rather I didn't?'

'It's just that we're here to talk about the importance of women being treated equally. I guess that means I should be able to manage my own luggage.'

'I won't tell, if you don't,' John said, as with the merest touch of hands Libby let go of the case, leaving John to carry it to the top of the stairs.

Moments later they were inside the lecture hall. An expansive room, lofty ceilings and picture windows running the length of one wall. The other walls featured a smattering of posters and notices. The writing was too small for Libby to read them from a distance, but she could see one was advertising the rock group, Cream. Another, Chuck Berry.

Many of the delegates had taken their place among the tiered seating. Others stood around in small groups, the buzz of quiet chatter appearing louder as it echoed around the spacious hall.

At the front of the hall was a raised platform where several women stood, the youngest of them with both hands on a microphone. The woman looked unsure of herself. She tapped the side of the microphone several times and appeared to speak into it, with no sound resulting from her attempts. And then, as if relieved the gadget could be abandoned, she laid it on the floor and clapped her hands, aiming to gain the attention of the audience.

'Welcome everyone. I'm Clem Richmond, one of the organisers of this weekend's debate. We're delighted to see so many of you here. We've got a busy weekend ahead of us, with a full agenda. And to make sure everyone has a chance to have their voice heard, we intend to divide into small groups, with myself and my colleagues here leading each of the sub-groups. You'll be in your small groups today, tomorrow and Saturday, then on Sunday we'll come back together to share our thoughts and hopefully make a plan of action. Remember, we are here not just to discuss what is possible, but to determine ways to make it happen. What's that saying? "Evil will triumph when good men do nothing," or something along those lines. You might argue that much of what women have had to suffer over generations can hardly be called "evil" but there are others who will tell you it's exactly what it's felt like to be constantly shoved to the bottom of the pile. I hope we'll all agree that change is needed and it's needed now, so let's get started.'

A muted chatter ensued, soon brought to an end with another of the organisers clapping her hands and calling for quiet.

'Let's keep this informal, shall we? Divide yourselves up into groups of eight or ten, and one of us will join you to facilitate. We'll be heading off to one of the classrooms down on the ground floor.'

All those who were previously seated stood at once, gathering handbags and coats and moving into the central aisle. There was a little confusion as some of the delegates headed towards the stage, while others headed towards the doorway. Then Clem Richmond, the only organiser who had introduced herself, took charge. Making her way to the double doors, she held a hand aloft, as if she was a conductor seeking the attention of an orchestra. No words were exchanged. Five delegates followed Clem out of the lecture hall, the last of which was John. Libby had noticed several men among the delegates, which was causing her some confusion. Wasn't this supposed to be a Women's Liberation conference? Nevertheless, she took Janie's hand, tugging her in Clem's direction.

Down on the ground floor, Clem led her little group along the corridor and into one of the classrooms. She laid her tattered leather satchel down on one of the desks and pulled out a manilla folder, stuffed full of papers.

'Grab a chair.' She nodded towards a stack of plastic chairs and moments later Libby, Janie and the rest of the group were seated in a semi-circle, looking expectantly at Clem, waiting for her to open the discussion.

Libby hadn't given much thought as to who might be organising the weekend. Nevertheless, she was mildly surprised that Clem looked to be a similar age to herself and Janie, early twenties at a guess. Tall and thin, Clem's hand-knitted jumper hung off her shoulders, making her look thinner still. What could be seen of her hair, from beneath her beret, fell in unruly waves, stopping just below her ears.

'Let's start with a quick introduction, shall we?' Clem nodded towards one of the women sitting on the far right of the semi-circle, who promptly stood up.

'Olivia Blythe,' she said, immediately sitting again.

Olivia's tone of voice, stylish clothes and expertly coiffured hairstyle, suggested she might have been more comfortable with a glass of dry sherry in her hand, while celebrating a mixed doubles win at Wimbledon. Refined, comfortable in her own skin. Surely part of the establishment they were all here to rail against.

By stark contrast, the next person to speak had to repeat her name several times before anyone could catch it. She gave her name as Bryony, and her refusal to raise her head, combined with her long hair hanging loose around her face, meant her voice disappeared into her blouse. A blouse Libby noticed was more than grubby around the collar.

Clem introduced Alison Newman, explaining that Alison would be sharing valuable insights regarding equality as they moved on through the weekend. Clem's tone suggested the group was lucky to have Alison in their midst. Meanwhile, Alison smiled and looking faintly embarrassed. While Clem considered the group were lucky, perhaps Alison felt less so.

Libby chose to introduce herself and Janie, leaving Janie nothing to say. 'We're here to listen and learn,' Libby said. 'I'm Libby Frobisher and this is my friend, Janie Juke. I write words and she reads them. Not mine exactly, but she's a librarian, so books are really her thing.'

Having uttered her unprepared summary that barely described their occupations, Libby looked around the group for some kind of acknowledgement. When none was forthcoming, she turned to Janie and shrugged.

The remaining members of the group yet to introduce themselves were men. Before they spoke Libby assumed the men had stumbled into the wrong room. During the Easter holidays the university facilities were bound to be used for other events. Events more likely to hold the attention of men.

The first of the two men to speak remained seated and, although his voice was confident, he held no one's gaze, choosing instead to look down at his feet. Bare feet inside worn leather sandals.

'Will,' he said, stopping as soon as he had started.

'I thought we were here to talk about being liberated from men? Should they even be included?' Libby said, glancing at Will, then at Clem.

'If we don't let men know what we hope to achieve, there's little chance we'll achieve it, is there?' was Clem's response, an undisguised edge to voice.

Everyone in the room fell silent and then, 'We're here to try to understand.' It was John's turn to justify their inclusion.

'Understand what, exactly?' Libby said. 'Surely there were no men at the Oxford conference? Isn't this a chance for women to air their views, without men elbowing in? We have to put up with enough of that the rest of the time, don't we, Janie?'

'You're wrong there, men did attend the Oxford conference. Some joined in the debate and others ran the creche. You might be surprised to learn that not all men are of one opinion,' Clem said. An attempt at humour, or a sarcastic jibe? Her expression gave nothing away.

'That's me put in my place,' Libby said.

'I do have some experience of what you women have to deal with,' John said, directing his words at Libby. 'My mum really wanted to join the Women's Peace Caravan, but with me as a littl'un, well, it stopped her. That's not an issue for men, if they want to do something, they go ahead and do it.'

'The Peace Caravan? What's that all about?' Libby asked.

'A group of women took off in an old army truck and a coach, headed for Soviet Russia, calling for nuclear disarmament,' Clem explained. 'So brave. A credit to womanhood.'

Clem paused, then chose to bring the room to order. 'Now the introductions are over, we'd best make a start.' Taking a marker pen, she quickly wrote the four discussion items for the weekend onto a whiteboard. 'We've a lot to get through and remember, it's important everyone has a chance to speak. We'll begin by sharing our views on the topics more generally. We'll stay in our small groups tomorrow and Saturday and talk in detail about each of the issues. Then on Sunday we'll join the rest of the delegates when we'll have an opportunity to outline our recommendations for change.'

Perhaps Clem had hoped the end of her introduction would lead directly into comfortable chatter. If so, she was to be disappointed. It seemed no one had a view, or if they did, they were loath to voice it.

'Equal pay.' Clem pointed to the first item on the whiteboard list. 'If a woman does the same job as a man she should receive the same wage. There can't be anything more straightforward.'

'Absolutely,' Olivia said.

'I can't imagine she's ever done a day's work in her life,' Libby whispered to Janie.

Janie nudged her friend into silence.

'We'll be discussing the importance of equal educational and job opportunities in more detail,' Clem said, pointing to the next two items on the list. 'We all know there's an equal amount of talent among women as men. In fact, some would argue women have keener brains, but time and again the routes to achievement are blocked. Take the team this university put up for last year's University Challenge. Three men and just one woman.' Thumping her fist on the whiteboard for emphasis, she paused to rub her hand, nursing the bruise that would soon appear.

'But they won, didn't they? Last year and three years ago. Quite brilliant they were.' The words were out before Janie had a chance to stop them. She'd told Libby often enough how much she loved

University Challenge and how she had cheered the Sussex team to victory.

'I think it's great that women want more equality,' John said, offering his best smile in Libby's direction.

'It's not about "more equality". Something is either equal or it isn't. And right now there is nothing that is equal for us,' Clem said. 'We have to shout loud and long until we rectify that.'

'You're right, Clem, but we're in the right place for these discussions,' Alison offered. 'This university has been leading the way, making a stand on the issues we all care about. When Sussex University opened a few years ago, there were twice as many female students as men.'

'Yes, well. Of course, there have been a few moves that take us in the right direction, but there's a long way to go before we see widespread change. Gentle persuasion and explanation are no longer enough.' Clem remained unimpressed. 'Let's not forget the other items on our agenda. Free contraception and abortion on demand, and free 24-hour nurseries. Until we can throw off the cloak of unwanted pregnancies, we will never be truly free. And for the mothers among us... well, if we're chained to domestic chores and bringing up baby, how can we ever pursue a career?'

'Crikey,' Libby said, directing her words at Clem. 'Sounds as if you'd like to turn the entire world on its head. Janie's a mum, but I doubt she sees herself as a domestic slave?' Posed as a question, Libby waited for her friend to respond, but she remained quiet.

Instead, Will's first contribution to the discussion resulted in everyone turning to look at him. 'Communes are the way to go, I reckon.'

'Free love, letting it all hang out, that kind of thing?' John said.

'I just mean everyone sharing responsibilities.' Will's response was prickly as he defended his opinion. 'Looking after the kids, growing food, providing shelter. I've seen it work really well.'

'Hippies?' Olivia said. 'That's fine, provided they don't leave their mess behind when they move on.'

'I think you're getting confused with travellers,' Alison chipped in.

'That's where he gets his fashion sense then,' Libby whispered to Janie, with a nod towards Will, whose bare feet, cheesecloth shirt, and Indian cotton trousers clearly met with her disapproval. 'And those sandals? It's not like it's summer.'

A bang on the table from Clem brought an end to the general conversation, as it was time to run through a few of the organisational arrangements for the weekend.

'A couple of general points to raise. All our visiting delegates have rooms in Block A of Park Village. I'm a student here at Sussex and I've kept my room on for the holiday. So, should you need to find me outside of our debating sessions, then you'll find me in Room 14, Block B. If I'm not there, stuff a note under the door and I'll catch up with you as necessary. And for those of you who have coats,' Clem glanced in Will's direction, 'you might as well keep them on because even if the sun shines, it won't alter the temperature in here; nothing as luxurious as an oil stove to make a difference,' Clem said.

'Perhaps the men who run this university are trying to tell us something,' Olivia said, directing her question at John and Will.

'Don't look at us,' Will said. 'We don't make the rules.'

'After supper, there will be free time to explore the university campus and to chat to the other delegates. Debating will start in earnest straight after breakfast in the morning, back in this classroom. So please don't dilly-dally, let's try to get going by nine o'clock. Remember, we have a real opportunity to influence. The Oxford conference was hailed as one of the biggest landmarks in British women's history. If we shout loud enough, we will surely make a difference.' Clem raised her voice to provide an example.

'There were around six hundred delegates at the Oxford conference. Do we really think anything we add will be worth listening to?' Libby said.

'Every voice is important,' Alison said, stepping in before Clem had a chance to respond.

'Should we take notes?' Bryony's first words since her initial introduction.

'Entirely up to you,' Clem said. 'I'm not here to tell you what to do or what to think. That's the whole point of a debate. Everyone's opinion is as valid as the next person's.'

For the next hour or so discussions continued, with the focus on equal pay for women.

'You do know those Dagenham women were paid less than the men who were sweeping the factory floor? And they were skilled, making the seat covers for men to put their bottoms on.' Olivia's tone was vehement, as if she was defending a relative.

'Seems there's more to Madam Olivia than first meets the eye,' Libby whispered to Janie.

'Where those striking women lead, we must follow,' Alison said.

'Here, here,' Clem said, her gaze scanning the others around the room, as if challenging them to disagree.

At that moment, John lent towards Libby and whispered in her ear. She was expecting him to share a comment about the striking women. Instead he said, 'Grab a seat for me at supper next to you and I'll tell you more about Mum's campaigning if you like. I reckon you've got attitude, just what's needed to achieve change.'

'Okay, I look forward to it.'

Libby watched John leave the room, sensing they had already made a connection.

CHAPTER 2

ONCE THE AFTERNOON SESSION had broken up, Janie and Libby had a chance to locate their bedroom for the first time. They dragged their cases across the campus, following the roughly drawn arrows directing them to the student digs in Park Village; an arrangement of three three-storey buildings, set around a central grassed area. As directed, they made their way to the building furthest from Falmer House; Student Block A. While all the rooms were occupied during term-time, the majority of students vacated their rooms during the holiday period, leaving them free for visitors.

They had just one flight of stairs to tackle before finding their room, half-way along the corridor. Once inside, Janie surveyed the spartan arrangement of the room. Two single beds covered with the thinnest of blankets; the only other furniture, a couple of chairs and a small table, with a lamp on it that was missing a light bulb. Without discussion, Libby chose the bed to the left of the table that sat under the window, sighing as she heaved her case onto the bed. Then she plumped herself down beside it, and offered her opinion on what had transpired so far. 'It all sounds pretty intense, doesn't it? I know these issues are important, but it's not as though all men are women-haters. Take John, for example.'

Even as Libby spoke, she was ready for Janie's disapproval. 'Just a quick reminder. We're here to debate serious women's issues, not to flutter our eyes at any available man. Remember, you're already spoken for. How is Ray?'

'Stop being a spoilsport and hold these for me.' Libby had opened her case to reveal a bottle of Spanish Sauterne and two plastic mugs, nestled in among her clothes.

'Are we allowed alcohol?'

'What we do in our own room is no one's business. We're liberated women, remember. Good job I remembered the corkscrew. I couldn't risk glasses, so we'll have to put up with drinking from these. After the first glass, you won't even notice.' Filling both mugs, Libby handed one to Janie.

'Toothbrush mugs?'

'Don't worry, the minty taste will add a little *je ne sais quoi*. Cheers and here's to a wild few days.'

'I'll drink to that, although how wild it will be remains in doubt.' Janie held out her empty mug. 'Top up?'

'Blimey, you knocked that back.'

'I've got a good excuse. First time for a long time, I don't have to be responsible.'

'I don't need an excuse. I've never been responsible.'

'Never a truer word. And please tell me, why have you brought so many clothes?'

Libby had spread the contents of her case out across the bed and was mulling over how best to hang them, given there was no wardrobe and only one double hook behind the door.

'A girl has to look her best, even at a women's lib do.'

'The clue is in the name of the weekend – women's liberation – we're supposed to be liberating ourselves from outdated ideas. The idea of dressing up to impress a man is straight out of a Jane Austen novel.'

'I can see you have no intention of impressing anyone, given that you have little more than a nightie in that case of yours.'

By the time they took their seats around the dining table an hour later, the bottle of Spanish Sauterne was almost empty, resulting in

Janie's overwhelming urge to giggle, which she managed to suppress by taking deep breaths.

Several tables had been prepared with cutlery, glasses, and jugs of water. Many of the delegates were already seated, choosing to stay with their sub-group companions from the afternoon session. Janie and Libby spotted Clem at one of the tables and made their way to join her. Bryony and Olivia sat on either side of Clem, with Will next to Bryony. Janie took the seat to the right of Libby, while Alison went to sit on her left.

'I'm keeping that for John,' Libby said, putting a hand on the chair. Even as she said the words, she realised how childish they sounded, as if she was back at school, hoping to curry favour with the most popular girl in class.

'Oh,' Alison said, moving to the next chair along.

'It's just that he said he'd tell me more about his mum. About the Peace Caravan.' An apology didn't help to shift the embarrassment.

A long counter ran along one wall of the refectory with an older woman and a teenage lad waiting to serve. Each table took it in turns to form a queue at the counter, collecting a plate onto which slices of spam coated in mostly charred breadcrumbs were added, together with a spoonful of boiled potatoes.

When their turn came, Libby and Janie stood in line behind Clem.

'John will have to suffer cold spam fritters unless he gets a move on,' Clem said.

'If they'd told us we'd be on army rations I'd have packed more than a Kit-Kat each,' Libby whispered, gazing down at her plate.

Olivia held her plate out and then appeared to have second thoughts. 'I think I might give it a miss, I'm not that hungry, anyway.' She put her empty plate down on the counter and returned to the table. 'We have to watch our figures, girls, don't we?' she said as the others returned.

It seemed no one agreed, or at least chose not to voice their agreement.

'We're here for serious debate, remember, not for the cuisine.' Clem said in a no-nonsense tone.

'And you won't let us forget that, will you?' Olivia said, her glare not going unnoticed by Libby.

General chatter between Alison and Janie broke the ensuing silence, Janie asking Alison more about her experience with women's rights.

'Clem exaggerated. I joined her on a couple of protest marches, nothing truly radical. She's the real activist.'

Much later that weekend Janie revisited Alison's words, but just then the talk of activism barely registered. She'd read about recent campaigns where hundreds, sometimes thousands, railed against nuclear armaments, or the war in Vietnam. Her friend Zara had spoken often about the injustice in the world and how everyone needed to stand up and be counted. It seemed Alison and Clem had done just that.

'How long have you two known each other?'

'Since schooldays. But we've only recently got back in touch. You know how it is…'

Janie nodded, sensing there was more Alison might have said if the others weren't listening.

With most plates cleared, it was time to return to the counter for the dessert offering, a choice between a banana or an apple. Some of the other delegates had already eaten and left the refectory. Each time the doors opened Libby turned in expectation. The empty seat beside her felt like a snub, as if she had been stood up on a hoped for first date.

'Where did John say he was going? Did he speak to you, Will?' Clem asked.

'No idea. But you know John. I'll go check his room if you like,' he said, leaving the refectory without waiting for a response.

'If he's found somewhere decent to eat, or even better a local pub, at least he could have told the rest of us about it,' Libby whispered to Janie. 'A couple more drinks might go some way to help us sleep on those concrete beds. And you'd better be telling me the truth when you say you don't snore.'

'I do not snore,' Janie said, loud enough to gain the attention of the others. 'Anyway, I'll be sleeping like a baby, concrete beds notwithstanding,' she continued, lowering her voice. 'I had two nights on the folding bed before I came away, remember.'

'After your row with Greg?' Libby said.

'It wasn't a row, more of a disagreement.'

'Maybe he would benefit from joining in this weekend's debate,' Libby said, receiving a quizzical look from Janie. 'Equality and all that. Liberating you from the chains of motherhood.'

'I have no desire to be liberated from anything, especially not Michelle. Greg and I have different views on certain things, that's all.'

'Marriage? The role of women?'

'Let's leave it, shall we?' Janie said.

'I'm just saying.'

'What are you saying, exactly?' Janie stood, pushing her chair back with more force than intended, sending it flying backwards.

'Perhaps you two could confine your fervour to tomorrow's debate,' Clem announced, taking a bite of her apple.

'Out of interest, Clem, your name?' Libby turned to Clem. 'That's short for...?'

'Clementine. I was born in December. My parents clearly had a sense of humour.' Her response was direct and unemotional. 'See you all for breakfast. Eight o'clock sharp.' And with that, she left the refectory.

Janie and Libby stayed for a while at the table, Libby silently hoping Will would return with some news of John. By the time Will came back in, everyone else had left and the kitchen staff were cleaning down the serving counter.

'He's not in his room,' Will said.

'He's gone off to find a pub, I'll bet,' Libby said. 'How about we do the same thing? You up for that, Will? We could grab a plate of chips to compensate for those spam fritters.'

'It's some distance to the nearest pub. I've only got my bike,' Will said.

'We'll take my car,' Libby said. 'Hang on while we get some bits from our room and we'll meet you downstairs.'

They grabbed their jackets from the back of their chairs and made their way across the campus to Park Village. Early evening in April rarely promised warmth, and this evening a chill had already set in, even before the sun had vanished from the skyline. Janie pulled a woollen scarf from her case, suggesting to Libby she do the same.

'I didn't bring one. Scarves are more your thing than mine.'

'For goodness sake. We're planning to go to the local pub, not parade down Carnaby Street. There'll be no one remotely interested in your dress sense. Like as not there'll be a few old men propping up the bar, a few workmen loitering over a pint to avoid having to read their son or daughter a bedtime story.'

'Spoken like a disgruntled mother?'

Janie was well aware of the fine line she was treading. Not only between her role as wife and mother and her job as a librarian. Her recent forays into amateur sleuthing had further complicated matters and often left her and Greg on opposite sides.

As well as feeling conflicted about her marriage, this was her first time away from her daughter. The first night she wouldn't be there to hold her while she had her last feed, tuck her up in her cot and sing her favourite nursery rhyme. This weekend away was a test for Janie, to decide what she wanted from life and work out how best to achieve it.

When they joined Will, it was clear he had finally succumbed to the weather, adding a brown woollen poncho over his thin shirt. The three of them presented an unusual set of companions. From the rear, Will could have been easily mistaken for a girl, his blonde hair long and loose down his back, his tie-dyed cotton trousers shades of pink and purple. Janie had chosen comfort over style, with her duffel coat and warm scarf suited to a countryside stroll. Libby, ever stylish in a houndstooth jacket, over her favourite polo sweater and mini skirt. Skirt lengths were a constant fascination for Libby, with the new midi and maxi styles gracing the catwalks in Paris and London. Once the designer fashions filtered down to local boutiques at a price she could afford, she would give them serious consideration.

The road from the car park led north from the campus. For about half a mile it was little more than a single track lane, no room even for two small cars to pass. On either side of the track the ground dipped away. Dusk had fallen and Libby was relying on the car headlights to guide her, to prevent her from veering too close to the edge. Now and then she muttered under her breath, slowing each time there was the merest curve in the road.

'Perhaps this wasn't such a good idea, after all,' Janie said. 'You've already had half a bottle of wine, remember?'

Janie's comments made Libby grip the steering wheel more tightly. Will sat in the back with his eyes closed, humming a tune.

'*Bridge over Troubled Water*?' Janie said.

'Yep, can't get it out of my head. I've just about got the chords nailed.'

'Guitar?'

'Yep, been playing for a while now.'

'Hopefully you'll give us a rendition later?'

The conversation appeared to bypass Libby, who remained focused on the narrow track ahead.

Once over the crossroads, the road widened, edged either side with a grassy verge and open fields, which soon gave way to dense woodland. Clumps of trees, mostly beech and silver birch, appeared from the shadows as the car headlights temporarily swept away the darkness.

As evening set in, the wind picked up, making the nearby tree branches bend low enough to almost touch Libby's car.

'Are we anywhere near the pub yet?' Libby asked, the first words she had spoken for some time. 'If not, I'd as soon turn around and head back.'

'Not much further. Once we're through the woods, it's another mile or so and we'll reach *The Royal Oak*,' Will said.

'Libby's least favourite pastime is driving,' Janie explained. 'So her offer to chauffeur us to the pub gives us an indication of her priorities in life.'

'Alcohol and chips?' Will said.

'And good-looking fellas,' Janie said, about to nudge Libby, before remembering her friend's total focus on the road ahead would mean she was deaf to Janie's teasing.

'It's such a shame you can't see these woods in daylight,' Will continued. 'I spent some of my happiest days round here as a kid. We were always being told to steer clear, but you know what it's like, when you're a kid and you're told not to do something, it makes you want to do it even more.'

'You grew up near here?' Janie asked.

'Yep. The place is quite beautiful all through spring and summer. The light green of the leaves of the beech trees shimmering in the sun, casting shadows on the bark of the silver birches. It's like a painting.'

'A poet as well as a musician?' Janie said.

Will gave a chuckle. 'The Canadians had a base here in the war. There are still notices up warning, "Danger Keep Out. MOD property", which makes it kind of weird. In a month or so they'll be thousands of bluebells, a thick carpet of them, then you see the notices and it seems impossible to imagine war ever existed here.'

As they approached a sharp hairpin bend, Libby slowed to an almost standstill. She guided the car around the bend, letting the headlights shine momentarily onto a clearing between the trees.

'Libby, stop the car. I think I just caught sight of something.' Janie peered through the windscreen into the gloom while Libby drew the car onto the grass verge, pulling on the handbrake.

'What? I can't see a thing, only trees.'

'As we went round that bend, I'm sure I saw something in the clearing over there.' Janie pointed into the near distance, opened the car door, and got out, with Libby and Will following close behind.

'I'm not sure about this, Janie. Will was just telling us this is an old MOD site. I don't much fancy wandering around in the dark, running the risk of stepping onto an unexploded bomb.' Clearly, Libby had been listening after all.

As the chill wind whipped through the trees Janie wrapped her scarf tighter around her shoulders, tucking the ends beneath the collar of her jacket.

'Look at you, you're shivering,' Janie said, linking her arm through Libby's.

'It's not from the cold, more from the fear of being blown to pieces. Who suggested this was a good idea, anyway?' Libby said.

Will was ahead of them, stepping cautiously over the uneven ground. 'Watch out, the path isn't very smooth. Don't go tripping up or we'll really be stuck. I can't drive, so it'll be a long walk back to get help.'

Clinging tightly to Janie, Libby edged forward, keeping a few steps behind Will. Only Janie had footwear suited to the woodland track. It wasn't only leaves that caught in Will's open-toed leather sandals, but the occasional spiky twig, causing him to pause every now and then to remove the offending item. Libby's beloved go-go boots made walking on uneven ground easy enough, but were unlikely to remain white by the time she returned to the car. Now and again she looked down at them, anxious the moss and damp grass would stain and they would be ruined.

'We should have brought a torch. I don't suppose you keep one in that car of yours?' Will called out to them.

Stepping further into the clearing, Janie could see a dark shape ahead, but was struggling to identify it. Then, another car passed by on the road behind them, briefly casting its headlights over the scene.

'Over there, look. Up against that tree. That's a weird place to park a car?'

They moved forward more quickly, forgetting the tricky ground underfoot. The front of the car was up against the trunk of one of the beech trees, the driver's door open, the car's front bumper askew. Even in the darkness they could see ruts in the ground where the car had come off the road, skidding to a stop only as it hit the tree.

'That's John's car,' Libby said, standing beside the open door and peering into the dark empty space inside.

'How do you know it's his?' Janie asked.

'Because I saw him get out of it in the car park. When we arrived, he was just ahead of us.'

'Are you certain? I don't remember seeing it.'

'Orange bodywork, black top. It might be dark, but I can see enough to tell you for definite it's his. I'm paid to be observant, remember?' It wasn't irritation Janie could hear in her friend's voice, but anxiety. 'He's had an accident, hasn't he? That's why he didn't come back for supper. He's probably lying somewhere bleeding to death and no one's even bothered to look for him.'

'Calm down and don't jump to conclusions,' Will said. 'He's not here, so he must have been okay enough to get out of the car and walk away.'

'If he walked away, where is he? He would have made his way back to the campus, wouldn't he? But he didn't come back, so that only leaves two possibilities, either he's lying somewhere unconscious, or he's dead.'

CHAPTER 3

WHEN JANIE, LIBBY, AND Will entered Falmouth House after finding John's car abandoned, Janie was already reflecting on the whys and wherefores of the event.

They had stayed beside the car for a while, calling out John's name, sensing even as they did so that it was highly unlikely he would suddenly emerge. It was too dark for a thorough search of the immediate area, so a mutual decision was made to return to the university to alert the others. For the whole return journey Libby posed questions about John's disappearance that neither Janie nor Will could answer.

Janie could tell Libby had developed a fascination for John, despite the brief time they had spent together. She knew her friend well enough to recognise the signs. And once emotions were in the mix, any serious conversation about the incident was bound to be tricky. In the past Libby had helped her unpick the circumstances behind a missing person incident. John's disappearance may be nothing of the sort, but if it was, then objectivity was critical.

Half way through the return journey Janie decided to try nudging Libby into a different frame of mind. 'You know he's married, you've seen the wedding ring, surely?'

'You disappoint me, Janie, you haven't grasped the concept of equality at all. Why can't I have a friendship with a man without people assuming it means something else? John strikes me as someone I would have things in common with, he'd be interesting to talk to about fashion, music too probably.'

'And you know that from the half a dozen words he's said to you?'

'Janie, you might be married, but don't tell me you're not aware of a good-looking fella. What about Davy Jones from The Monkees?'

'He's not real though is he? I mean he's not someone I'm ever likely to bump into or have a conversation with. He's a pop star, for goodness' sake.'

'Just try to keep an open mind. That's all I'm saying.'

Will appeared to be unaware of the conversation going on between driver and passenger, as he remained silent throughout. Janie couldn't see his expression, but she got the sense there was more troubling him than finding John's car.

As they stepped into Falmouth House, the reception area was lit up, but the refectory was in darkness. Pushing open the double doors, Will flicked the light switch, bringing a cold fluorescent brightness to the empty room.

'Looks like they've all taken themselves to bed,' he said.

'We'll have to wake them up,' Libby said, an urgency in her voice. 'Clem at least. We'll need to phone the police and once they're involved Clem will have to bring the weekend to a close. We can hardly carry on as if nothing's happened.'

Janie led the way down the footpath and across the campus to the student digs. She recalled Clem mentioning the location of her bedroom should they need to find her. Determined to move things along at pace, Libby marched forward and banged on Clem's bedroom door. A second or two later the door opened. Clem was wearing a candlewick dressing gown over a long pink nightie. The slippers on her feet reminded Janie of slippers her mother used to wear, pink and fur-lined. The way Clem dressed for bed was so at odds with the person who had addressed the group earlier that day that the three of them fell silent.

Then Libby said, 'It's John.'

'What about him?' Clem said.

'We found his car abandoned in the woods, north of here. Will knows the area, he'll explain exactly where.' Libby held her arms out as if pleading for answers.

'We don't know if he's hurt,' Janie explained. 'But it looks as though he's come off the road somehow, and crashed the car into a tree ...'

'And no sign of him?' Clem said, holding the door open a little as she stood on the threshold. The others remained side-by-side in the corridor.

'But his keys are still in the ignition,' Libby said. 'So it doesn't look good whichever way you look at it.'

'Let's not to jump to conclusions,' Clem said.

'We called out, in case he was anywhere nearby,' Janie said. 'But it was dark, we didn't have a torch...'

'I'd say that's a good thing,' Clem said. 'I mean, if he was badly hurt he wouldn't have been able to go far. If you couldn't find him, he must have been well enough to walk away. You'll probably find he's made his way home. Look, you'd better come into my room, no point us all standing here in the corridor.'

They stepped into Clem's bedroom, a room identical to the one Janie and Libby shared, but with one bed rather than two. Even the desk lamp was unlit, perhaps it too was missing a bulb. Across the desk handwritten papers were scattered, alongside two piles of books. Janie scanned a few of the titles. A Vindication of the Rights of Women sat on top of one pile of text books that appeared to be championing the topics Clem was passionate about. The other pile included Jane Eyre and several books by Virginia Woolf. Despite being familiar with the fictional titles from her work in the library Janie had never read any Woolf. Nevertheless, she knew enough about the author's tragic life to appreciate her struggles with depression, contrasting with her great literary talent. Did a person's reading habits provide an insight into their character? A question Janie could pose at herself and one that her closest friends and family might each have a different answer to.

'Tell me again exactly what you found,' Clem said.

Janie ran through the details again while the others remained silent. Libby stayed in the doorway, as if she needed to be ready to spring into action.

'And the keys were still in the ignition?'

'Yep,' was Will's only contribution to the conversation. Although silent, Will's expression suggested he was having some kind of internal argument with himself.

'Well, I can't see the point in notifying the police at this stage. It'll be a waste of their time and they won't thank us for it.'

'What makes you say that?' Janie said.

'The police have their own agenda. They see us as troublesome women, nothing more,' Clem said. 'I've come up against them before, I know how they can be.'

'A man is missing, he could be hurt.' Janie was struggling to think of a reason not to notify the police. 'At the very least we should ring round the local hospitals. Someone might have picked him up and driven him there.'

'It'll be the County Hospital in Brighton if he's been taken anywhere. But my thoughts are that alcohol can leave people disorientated, confused. I bet he's headed off to the pub, had several too many, careered off the road and crashed into the tree. Someone will have passed by and picked him up. He's local, he knows loads of people round here. You mark my words, right now he'll be home nursing a thick head.'

Janie noticed Will becoming increasingly distressed. She could hear his breathing, shallow and fast-paced.

'No,' he said, shaking his head. 'We found John's car in Barcombe Woods. There's no pub between here and there. He's come off the road before he had a single drink. And why would he leave his keys in the car? It doesn't make sense.'

The words fell heavily in the room. It was as if each of them was waiting for someone else to suggest the next steps.

Clem was the first to speak. 'Who spoke to John last night? Will, did he tell you he was going home?'

'He said nothing to me,' Will said. 'I think he was more interested in chatting to Libby.'

All eyes were on Libby.

'I've already told you, he just said he had to fetch something from his car. Nothing more. Let's at least ring the hospital. If someone found him, injured, they would have phoned for an ambulance, surely?'

'Shouldn't we ring his wife?' Will said. Janie could see he was still fretting.

'It's late,' Clem said. 'If we ring his wife and John isn't home, we'll make her anxious and maybe for no reason. He's just as likely to be sleeping it off on a friend's couch. He'll have plenty of people close by he could turn to.'

'Okay,' Janie said. 'I'm going to ring the hospital now and if that doesn't provide answers and if there's no news by the morning, I'll ring the police.'

'I'm certain this will turn out to be no more than a minor scrape and John will be right as rain,' Clem said. 'Now, if you don't mind I'll say goodnight. We've a busy day ahead of us tomorrow.' She held the door open, waiting for them to leave.

Once out in the corridor Janie was tempted to quiz Will in the hope that her hunch was right, that there was something worrying him about John's disappearance that he was choosing not to speak about.

'Do you think Clem is right?' she said.

'About John?'

'That we shouldn't worry about him, that he'll be just fine?'

Will's only response was to shrug and then, 'I'm off to bed. If you have any news from the hospital maybe you'll let me know? My room is on the same floor, three along from yours.' He was down the corridor and out of the main entrance before either of them could reply.

'How much loose change have you got?' she asked Libby once back in their bedroom.

They emptied their purses onto one of the beds for Janie to collect a selection of coins, which she shoved into her coat pocket.

'Shall I come with you?' Libby asked.

'No point us both going. I don't know which will be worse, if he's been hurt, or if they say they have no record of him, which would leave us no further forward.'

The phone box was located to the side of the central courtyard of Park Village. Trawling through the Yellow Pages she found the number for the casualty department of Brighton's main county hospital and rang, to be told that no one in the name of John Bramber had been admitted. Tempted as she was to ring the police there and then, she decided against it. Something about this wasn't right. It was as if she had been presented with a tangled ball of wool and had to determine which thread to catch hold of to unravel it. Perhaps the morning would bring a solution.

Janie had woken early, pulling the blinds back to let the milky morning sunshine flood into the room. She sat up in bed for a while, listening to Libby's gentle breathing. If she woke her friend now, there might just be time to drive out to Barcombe Woods, to take a look at John's car in the daylight. She checked her watch. Clem had told them breakfast would be served at eight sharp. By the time they'd washed, dressed and driven out there they'd have little time to make a thorough search of the area. Perhaps it was better to drive out there later, after the first morning session. Although she was still holding out hope that John would stroll into breakfast, ready to explain his strange vanishing act to anyone prepared to listen.

But when they joined the others around the breakfast table John was still not in evidence. Apart from John's absence little had changed from the previous evening. It was almost as though the relative normality of the weekend conference had barely been disrupted by the disappearance of one of their group. Olivia was the only one among them who seemed to be making a statement with her latest outfit, perhaps hoping for some words of admiration, even envy. The apple green knitted dress and matching long coat she had worn the day before had been replaced by a peach blouse, fringed suede mini skirt and knee-length boots. In another place, in different circumstances, Janie had no doubt Libby would be quizzing Olivia about her fashion choices, where she'd bought them and how high the price tag. But this wasn't the moment for any of that.

Bryony, Olivia and Alison remained unaware of the previous night's events. It was only when Olivia nodded towards John's empty chair that Clem explained.

'Sleeping in after a heavy night, is he?' Olivia said.

'They found John's car abandoned in Barcombe Woods,' Clem said.

Olivia was about to take a spoonful of cornflakes, but stopped mid-way. 'Goodness, really? Who found it?' Everything about her manner resembled someone in the front row of a theatre production, part of the audience waiting expectantly for the plot to unfold.

'We found John's car,' Janie said. 'Libby, Will and I. We went for a drive after supper.'

'And John?' Olivia said. 'He's alright?'

'He'll be fine,' Clem said. 'At home more than likely.' Her matter-of-fact statement a signal that for the moment the topic was closed. 'Our first debate will start in ten minutes, so eat up and I'll see you in the room we were in yesterday.' She stood, pushed her chair away from the table and left the refectory, most of her breakfast remaining uneaten.

'That's us told then,' Libby said.

All the time they'd been seated around the breakfast table, Janie noticed that every time there was a noise Libby turned to look in the direction of the door, as if still hoping John would suddenly walk in. Where could he be? What might have happened to him?

Will had asked to join them on the drive. A request made in all innocence perhaps, although Janie knew too well how effectively people could hide their true intentions. After supper the previous evening Will had offered to look for John, to check his room to see if he had gone straight there without coming in for supper. Will was gone for quite a while. Perhaps he had found John, and the two of them had had an argument, a violent disagreement that left John racing off. Distracted by anger, or frustration John could easily have lost control of his car. Then, once Will's temper had subsided, he may have wanted to make sure John was okay, no harm done.

All of it was supposition. Right now Janie could do no more than observe and take mental notes as the morning unfolded.

At nine 'o'clock the morning's debate got underway, with Alison opening the discussion.

'As Clem mentioned, this morning we're going to focus on equal pay for women.'

'Or lack of it,' Libby said.

'Indeed. First, a brief history lesson. Working women have been treated unfairly for decades,' Alison continued.

'Centuries, more like,' Libby said.

'You're right, Libby. Much of it you will already know. Women have long been straining to make their voices heard. As far back as 1918, at the end of the Great War, there was a strike by women working on the trams and buses. They'd stepped in to help when the men were off fighting, yet the bosses, in their wisdom, decided not to pay them the same wage as the men had been earning.'

'It sickens me to think how many women have been mistreated,' Clem said. 'And every woman who doesn't use her voice for change is complicit. We'll only succeed if we stand together.'

It was difficult to read the glance from Alison, but then she continued. 'There was the suffragette movement, of course, and the terrible hardships they endured to get us the vote. But having the vote only means something if the people we vote for have women's interests at the forefront of their policies.'

'Look at how few women there are in government today,' Clem added. 'Twenty-six female members of Parliament out of what – more than six hundred? No wonder we aren't being listened to.'

'Hang on though,' Will chipped in. 'There'll be men who support women's rights too.'

'That's right. Look at how passionately John spoke yesterday about his mum,' Libby said, her anxieties resurfacing again.

'Let's refocus for a minute,' Alison said. 'It's not all gloom and doom. We have Barbara Castle fighting our corner. And with debates and conferences like these across the country, we have more of a chance our voices will be heard. It's critical we continue to shout loud and strong.'

'The trouble is most bosses are men,' Janie said. 'So if they set the wages, they're bound to favour their own kind, aren't they?'

'That's why we need legislation,' Alison said. 'That way employers won't have a choice. The more we campaign the greater the chances we can force through change. Look at what Nancy Astor and Edith Summerskill managed to achieve during the last war. They came from different sides of the house in Parliament, yet they stood together on a platform in Trafalgar Square to demand the government pay equal compensation to women and men for war injuries. And it worked.'

'They were important, though. People aren't going to listen to the likes of us, are they?' Bryony's quiet voice provided such a contrast with Alison's eloquent oration that for a few moments there was silence.

Then Alison took up the thread once more. 'I'm a teacher. And, without wanting to boast, I reckon I'm a pretty good teacher. But for years I've received at least ten pounds less a year than my male colleagues. And it's not only about money, either. When I was interviewed for my first teaching job, the headmaster told me in no uncertain terms I could only keep the job if I remained single. "There's no place in teaching for married women," he announced. "Divided responsibilities. Once you're married, you'll be busy attending to the needs of your husband."'

A loud laugh from Janie changed the focus of the room away from Alison. 'You're not serious, surely? That sounds like something out of the last century.'

'Sadly, that opinion is all too common,' Clem said. 'You're married, Janie, aren't you? Has it stopped you from pursuing a career?'

'I'm a librarian and I love my job, but I'm not sure you'd call it a career.'

Janie knew she hadn't answered Clem's point entirely, but she had no intention of discussing the difficulties in her marriage with people she barely knew.

Janie had noticed her friend continually checking her watch and now it was as if she could no longer be silent.

'How long are we going to wait?' Libby said.

'Wait? What for?' Clem said.

'Until we have news of John. Janie, we need to ring the police now. We shouldn't delay any further.'

'I saw him drive off.' Bryony's contribution seemed to come from nowhere.

'Last night? You saw John drive off? Why didn't you say something before now?' Clem's exasperation led Bryony to hide her face behind her hair so her response was barely more than a mumble.

'What did you see, Bryony?' Janie tried a gentler tone aiming to encourage a fuller explanation.

'Just before we came through for supper. I popped outside for a ciggie,' Bryony said. 'I saw him pulling away.'

'Which direction?' Clem again.

Bryony offered a shrug by way of reply.

'Clem, do you think this might be a good time for a short break?' Alison said.

'Let's say, half an hour,' Clem said. 'A walk around the grounds. Then we'll return refreshed.'

Janie nudged Libby. 'First, I'm going to ring Dad, see how Michelle is.'

The short walk to the phone box near the entrance to Park Village, gave Janie time to gather her thoughts. She dialled the number and within a couple of rings she heard her dad's voice.

'Hello love, are you having a good time?'

From her earliest memories Janie equated her dad's soothing tone with safety, reassurance, and love. The bond between them had always been rock solid, made even more special when Janie's mother walked out on both of them shortly after her dad's accident.

'Dad, is Michelle okay?'

'Michelle is just wonderful. Your Aunt Jessica has been making such a fuss of her I wouldn't be surprised if she asks you to leave her with us permanently.'

'Ha, I don't think so. Seriously though, what about Greg? Did he come round for supper last night? Is he okay?'

'Janie, we're all fine here. But you sound a bit tense. Is there a problem?'

A brief run down was all that was needed for Philip Chandler to grasp his daughter's concerns.

'I'll admit it sounds a bit strange. But I'm sure there's a straightforward explanation. You could be right, probably someone saw him near to the woods after the accident, picked him up and drove him home. You say the hospital had admitted no one by that name?

'That's right. I'll leave it a bit longer, but if we don't hear anything soon, I'll ring the police.'

'And why doesn't the organiser want you to involve them? Her name's Clem, you say?'

'Think a seventies version of Emmeline Pankhurst, and you won't be far wrong.'

'Strong views, then?'

'You aren't kidding. But there's something else, Dad. One of the girls, Bryony, she's really shy, barely says anything. She said she saw John drive away when she went for a cigarette before supper.' Janie hesitated while she clarified her thoughts. 'The thing is, I'm pretty sure she doesn't smoke.'

'What makes you say that?'

'Earlier Clem and Alison – she's the teacher I mentioned - they were both outside chatting and as Bryony passed by Clem offered her a cigarette and she shook her head. I heard her say, "No thanks, I don't."'

'I wouldn't read too much into that. She might be hoping to cut down, or even give up, but she had a weak moment. Anyway, why would she say she'd gone for a smoke if she hadn't?'

'Exactly.'

'Dad, my money's going to run out. Give Michelle a big kiss from me and Jessica too and I'll ring again tomorrow.'

'Let me know how you get on,' were Philip's final words before the pips signalled the end of the call.

Janie had barely put the receiver down when Libby was there tugging the phone box door open.

'There's been a development,' Libby said, her cheeks flushed.

'What?'

'Will was on about ringing John's wife to see if he was at home.'

'And is he?'

'That's the point, Janie. A phone message has just come through from John's wife, something about his work. John isn't at home. No one knows where he is.'

CHAPTER 4

THE UNIVERSITY'S STUDENT DIGS in Park Village had first opened to students barely six months earlier. The development had already been hailed as a great success, some saying it would form the blueprint for student accommodation across the country. There were three floors to each building, the village housing some three hundred bedrooms in total. Students had access to communal kitchens and bathrooms and eventually the village would include a common room and bar.

Greg's sister, Becky, had been a student at Sussex for just two terms. When she learned Libby and Janie were going to be staying on the university campus, she regaled them with a host of anecdotes about her time there. For Janie, the most surprising revelation was that Becky and most of her student friends sat on the floor in the corridor of one student house or another to eat their meals, with a plate on their lap.

'What, there are no tables or chairs?' Janie asked her.

'It doesn't matter, we don't care,' was Becky's reply. 'When you're a student, you let it all hang out. That's the great thing about it.'

'Have you told your mum and dad?' Janie wanted to know. Mr and Mrs Juke weren't the most progressive thinking couple. She could imagine heated discussions were commonplace in the Juke household as Becky explored a new and independent life.

'There's no point, they wouldn't understand. They're oldies,' was Becky's pronouncement on her parents.

Libby's reaction when she heard about it, was one of envy. 'Imagine the fun they're having. You and I missed out on all that, more's the pity.'

'Aren't they supposed to be studying? Isn't that more the point of it, rather than drinking and partying until the small hours and sleeping in all morning to recover?'

'You can be such a square sometimes, Janie,' Libby said, leaving Janie smarting a little. 'Anyway, if you remember, it was down to you that Becky moved into the student digs. She was about to move into a house with Oliver Mowbray until you intervened.'

Rightly or wrongly, Janie couldn't be bothered to think of a reason to disagree with Libby. Both were spending the half-hour break following Becky's example; sitting on the floor of their twin-bedded room, sharing a Kit-Kat, reflecting on what to do next regarding John's disappearance.

'What did your dad say?' Libby said, crumpling up the silver paper and licking the chocolate from her fingers.

'He agrees with us that the whole thing seems strange, including Clem's reaction to the police.'

'Did you hear a knock on our bedroom door last night?'

'I was out for the count. You moaned at me for snoring, remember? Why? You don't think it was John, do you?'

'I don't know what to think.'

'You seem genuinely concerned about him, Libby, but you hardly know him.'

'I'd be upset about anyone disappearing like that. You would too if you weren't so caught up feeling guilty about leaving Greg. Come on, Janie, we're a team, aren't we? We've been successful tracking down a missing person before, let's approach this with a clear head and make a plan.'

'I've been thinking the same thing. But I've been worried you'd lost your objectivity, worrying about John for the wrong reasons.'

'There are no wrong reasons. Just because I think John seems like a nice bloke, it's not going to colour my judgement. You cared about Zara, remember, but it didn't stop you from getting to the truth.'

'Sorry, you're right, and by way of an apology you can have the last finger of Kit-Kat.' Handing over the chocolate, Janie stood and tipped out the contents of her bag onto her bed. 'Look, I've even brought my notebook.'

She sat back down beside Libby and turned to a clean sheet in her notebook, heading it, 'John Bramber, Missing.' 'That's a start, I suppose. What next?'

Before Libby could reply, there was a knock on the door to which Libby called out, 'Come in.'

The door opened to reveal Alison. Janie tried to imagine Alison leading a class of children. Alison hadn't said if she taught primary or secondary, but something about her demeanour made Janie think she would gain respect from any and all ages. She could only guess at Alison's age, but reckoned she was a similar age to Clem. Yet Alison's sensible court shoes and twin set suggested a stability, a gentle authority that might come from someone who had enjoyed a lifetime as a teacher. A natural then. Someone who had found the perfect niche early on in her career, which left Janie feeling a little envious.

Alison remained in the doorway, looking down at Libby and Janie, who were both looking up at her.

'Is it okay if I come in?'

'Yes, of course. Just ignore us sitting on the floor, we're getting into the student vibe,' Libby said, winking. 'Sit on the bed if you like. In fact, I think we'll all be more comfortable sitting on the bed, even though the idea of a sprung mattress is far too modern for Park Village.'

Alison sat on the edge of Libby's bed, her long patchwork skirt covering short legs and stubby ankles. Perhaps it was her short, round stature, her motherly appearance, which gave her the air of a person who children would happily turn to for reassurance.

Janie and Libby settled themselves side-by-side on Janie's bed and waited for Alison to speak.

'You should have seen the place when the first lot of students moved in last summer,' Alison said. 'Most of it was still a bomb site, literally. Piles of bricks and rubble everywhere, scaffolding covering just about every building, not that it seemed to bother the students.'

'You're right there,' Janie said, swinging her legs up underneath her and pushing herself back to lean against the wall. 'My sister-in-law started here as a student last summer and she couldn't be more thrilled with the whole student experience. Builders, scaffolding, all of it seemed to pass her by.'

'I'm developing a mental list of complaints,' Libby said, trying to lighten the mood for her own sake. 'No irons, no full-length mirrors, not a single one. How's a girl supposed to manage?'

'Sorry, Alison, you'll have to excuse Libby's rather warped sense of humour. But on a serious note I'm hoping you're here with news about John?' Janie said.

'No news, except to say Clem is keen for us to carry on with the conference.'

'Surely not?' Libby said. 'When the police turn up they might think differently.'

'Have you rung them yet?' Alison asked.

'I'll wait until lunchtime, but no longer. I'm still hoping he'll just turn up, or at least that we'll have some news of him at least. Do you know who took the message from John's wife? Was it Clem?' Janie asked.

'No, it was Peter. The young kitchen hand. I'm guessing the woman on the switchboard tried various extensions and Peter was the only one to pick up.'

'I'm sorry, but I think we've got this all wrong,' Libby said, any remaining lightness vanished. 'Right now Mrs Bramber is assuming her husband is here at the university. Shouldn't she be told? And is that what you've come to tell us? That Clem wants to carry on with the conference?'

'There is something.' Alison stood and moved towards the door. 'It might be worth getting Will on his own?'

'Why are you telling us?' Libby asked.

'He's more likely to open up to you than he is to me.'

And with that Alison was gone, but not before reminding them that Clem was expecting everyone to reconvene as soon as possible for another short debate before breaking for lunch.

On their way from Park Village to Falmer House they saw Will ahead of them. He was deep in conversation with Bryony, which was a surprise in itself, but meant this was not the time to speak to him in private. Instead, as they came full circle around the building Olivia approached them.

'Do you have a minute?' Olivia said, holding her arm out, creating a temporary barrier to their entry back into the main building. Her long woollen coat clung to her and it was only now that Janie had the sense that Olivia's manner, her apparent confidence, was all a sham.

'I think Clem wants us all back in, doesn't she?' Libby said.

'Yes, yes, I know. But before we go in I wanted to tell you something. It's about John.' She dropped her voice to little more than a whisper.

'What about John?' Janie asked.

'Last night, before supper, I saw him, just over there.' Olivia pointed to the alleyway that led to the back kitchen entrance. 'He was talking to someone and the conversation looked very heated.'

'Did you hear any of the conversation?' Janie said.

'I was too far away to hear, but the other person was definitely angry, waving their arms around..'

'Why didn't you say something earlier?' Libby held steady eye contact with Olivia, neither flinching nor looking away.

'Olivia, it was still light before supper. Are you sure you couldn't see who the person was? Could it have been one of the other delegates?' Janie said.

'It's none of my business. I don't want to get involved.'

'Involved in what?'

'All I'm saying is that you're right to bring the police onboard, no matter what Clem says about it. Clem has her own opinions and is unlikely to be persuaded away from them. Certainly not by me,' Olivia said. 'Anyway, now I've told you, I'll leave you to decide what you do about it.' And with that she turned and climbed the steps into Falmer House.

'How weird was that?' Libby said. 'I thought the weekend was supposed to be a lesson in how to achieve equality. Right now, it feels as though there's one chief and a handful of timid Indians.'

CHAPTER 5

IT WAS HARD TO focus on the content of the late morning's debate. Janie felt like an observer, listening but not really hearing anything. Instead she studied each of the faces of the group around her.

Bryony kept her head bowed, clinging tightly to the little notepad resting on her knee, pencil poised. Clem's gaze was fixed on Alison, while Olivia seemed more interested in inspecting her varnished fingernails and repeatedly smoothing down the tassels that ran around the bottom of her skirt. Will's focus was towards the window and beyond, his expression suggesting that despite being physically present in the room, his thoughts were elsewhere.

'We are the luckiest generation,' Alison began. 'Last year plans were finalised for something they're going to call the Open University. It will revolutionise further education and will be open to everyone.'

'I've heard it's all going to be based in Milton Keynes,' Olivia said, appearing pleased she had something to contribute. 'You won't find me going there.'

'It's not called "open" for no reason,' Alison continued, ignoring Olivia's disparaging tone. 'When students enrol, they'll be sent course notes, books, even cassette tapes. You'll be able to study at home and they'll even have programmes on the BBC to support the learning. University education that is truly equitable, accessible to any and everyone.'

'You'll have to pay though, won't you?' Bryony said, lifting her head a little, while her hair continued to provide a curtain of privacy.

'There are costs involved,' Alison replied, 'but they are quite minimal. I think it's around twenty pounds for each module. And there'll be grants for people who might otherwise struggle, just like there are for standard university education. But don't you see, the difference with this type of learning is that you can still work, so you can fit it in around your day-to-day life.'

'Twenty pounds might not be a lot to you, but it's more than I earn in a week. It's okay for you with a teacher's salary, but all my wages go on food, on rent. After that there's nothing left.' There was passion in Bryony's tone that hadn't been heard until now.

'Alison mentioned grants, that could be worth exploring if you were thinking about applying. I'm in the same boat as you, Bryony,' Janie said. 'I don't earn much at the library, but I really like the idea of studying with a university without having to give up my job. Surely, any learning is never a waste, is it?'

'Janie is right,' Alison continued. 'This is a wonderful opportunity for us all, and so relevant to our debating topics this weekend. We all need to be more like Jennie Lee. She was a rebel who wouldn't be silenced.'

'Jennie Lee?' Janie wanted to know more.

'A Scottish miner's daughter who got herself a law degree back in the days when hardly any women went to university. She was voted into Parliament, aged twenty-three, when she wasn't even old enough to vote. Women had to be thirty before they could vote.'

'She sounds like my kind of person,' Libby said, clapping her hands. 'Brave enough to stand out from the crowd; breaking down barriers.' She directed her words at Clem who seemed temporarily lost for words and so Alison continued.

'Anyway, like I say, Jennie Lee was a rebel, along with her husband, Nye Bevan. And when Harold Wilson asked her to get involved with setting up this new concept for a "university of the air" she came up with the idea of calling it an Open University, a university where learning could be easily accessed with no impossible hurdles to jump over. And she fought everyone who said it was "blithering nonsense".'

'Good for her,' Will said, seeming to have only just tuned into the conversation. Janie followed Will's continued gaze, but couldn't see anything outside except a huge grey cloud in an otherwise bright blue sky.

Olivia had been quiet since her comment about Milton Keynes. Now she held her hand up as if to catch the group's attention.

'You don't need permission to speak, Olivia. We're not at school anymore,' Clem said, her tone contradicting her words.

'I read an interesting article about the work they're doing in Milton Keynes, preparing the new buildings there. Did anyone else read it? It's quite a funny story.'

Silence from the others led her to continue.

'It seems the site ended up being nothing but a sea of mud over the autumn last year and the Vice Chancellor was so worried about all the mud being trodden into the new carpets he told someone to go off and buy one hundred pairs of slippers for the staff to wear.'

'Ridiculous,' Clem blurted out, making them all turn towards her. 'For goodness' sake, that's exactly the kind of thing we have to expose for the madness it is.'

'Sorry, Clem, but I can't see what's wrong with it.' Olivia said, sounding hurt, as if she had been reprimanded. 'I wouldn't want my carpets ruined, would you? It seems eminently sensible to me.'

'Why are we even talking about material possessions, about how something looks?' Clem said. 'It's this focus on appearances that has hampered women down the ages.'

'I've never worn a pair of slippers in my life,' Will said, looking down at his bare feet.

'Do you reckon Clem has been unlucky in love?' Libby whispered. 'I mean, it might sound horrible, but really, with that haircut, a jumper that looks like she's wearing it inside out, and that sharp tongue of hers, not many men would be brave enough to get involved, would they?'

By the time they were ready to break for lunch the mood of the room had settled. Alison had finished her talk on the marvels of inclusive education and Janie was keen to ask her more about the ins and out of the Open University when she could catch her on her own. Working in the mobile library meant Janie had access to all the reading material she could want, but the idea of studying something in more depth held a real fascination for her. Her recent forays into criminal investigations – albeit from the sidelines - had left her wanting to know more about police procedure, the law, and everything else needed to achieve a successful criminal conviction. Perhaps this new university could offer her the chance to take the first slow steps towards a new career, while hanging on to her old one. Although, explaining her reasoning to Greg was likely to present a challenge.

'You're deep in thought,' Libby said, as they left the lecture hall. 'Penny for them?'

'Is there time to drive back up into the woods before lunch? I'd like to take another look at John's car in the daylight, to see if we missed anything last night that might tell us what happened to him.'

'Good idea, that way when you ring the police we might have a bit more detail to give them.'

This time as Libby drove slowly north, Janie was grateful for the chance to take in the surroundings. The previous evening a dull day had given way to an early dusk, followed quickly by darkness. But now, as they travelled the same route, she was able to enjoy the scenery, the small flock of sheep to one side, several of them nestling against the hedge that divided one field from the neighbouring one. After a wet winter, the grass was lush, offering plenty of grazing. Janie gave an exclamation of delight as two lambs, barely able to stand, nestled into their mother, one on each side.

They were headed towards the South Downs. A few years earlier the national park had been designated an Area of Outstanding Natural Beauty, and looking across the landscape she could understand why. If I could paint, this would be the perfect inspiration. Undulating chalk hills, covered with a mixture of meadow and farmland, offered unbroken views that extended for miles. In places it was as if the sky came down to meet the land, a marriage of two marvels of nature.

Even though the sun continued to hid behind the clouds, with the car windows closed, what little warmth it offered magnified the heat. Libby had thrown her jacket on the back seat before they set off, while Janie had kept her coat on and now wished she hadn't.

'I'll wind the window down if that's okay?' Janie said, doing so before her friend replied. The sound of the sheep baaing, combined with birdsong, could be heard over the sound of the engine and despite the reason for their journey Janie could sense a lightness in Libby's mood that hadn't been there since the previous evening, reinforced as Libby began to hum Bridge over Troubled Water.

Reminded of Will's rendition of the song the previous evening, Janie asked, 'What's your impression of Will?'

'He seems nice enough. Why? Do you think he's hiding something?'

'I do, yes. But I'm not sure if that "something" is relevant.'

'Why not come straight out and ask him?'

'Maybe I will.'

'Your dad is always telling you to trust your instincts, isn't he?'

Philip Chandler had supported his daughter through her previous investigations into three mysterious events that had occurred in their home town of Tamarisk Bay. As a result Janie was gaining confidence, while struggling to ignore her husband's disapproving comments. The two most important men in her life effectively sat on opposite sides of an unspoken argument, none of which helped her to decide how best to take her life forward.

They left the narrow track, the road opening up as it led through the woods. Janie sat up tall, scanning left and right.

'Slow down, Libby. Here, can you pull over?'

Libby guided the car onto a wide grassy verge, pulling it up and off the main carriageway.

'I'm pretty sure we're close. Let's do the rest on foot.'

Locking the car and crossing the road to take the path into the woods, Libby led the way.

'Come on, slow coach, what's keeping you?' Libby said.

'I'm unfit, that's what. I still haven't shifted the weight I put on when I was expecting. Look at this.' Janie grabbed a handful of flesh around her midriff. 'It's disgusting. I can't fit into hardly any of the clothes I was wearing before I was pregnant.'

'Keep fit classes, that's what you need. Come to the one I go to every Wednesday evening. You'll soon be slim and trim again, no problem.'

They had been walking for a few minutes when Janie stopped.

'I'm not sure we're in the right place. It all looks so different in daylight. I didn't think John's car was this far in. We might be in the wrong place.'

Beyond where they were standing the woodland track divided, the left-hand side mostly covered with brambles and nettles.

'We'll get ripped to pieces if we go that way,' Libby said, attempting to tread down a particularly spiky thread of nettles that crossed over the footpath. 'These boots will be ruined. I'll never get the grass stains off them.'

'A reminder that life is not always about strolling down a fashion catwalk.'

'That doesn't even deserve a response.'

'Forget about that for a minute, if we're on the right footpath, shouldn't we be able to see the car from here?'

As they surveyed their immediate surroundings, Janie had a sudden thought that the car may have been moved. It was entirely possible John had returned, picked up the car and driven home. A scenario that would mean he was okay. Nevertheless, she couldn't shake the feeling there would be no good news anytime soon.

After a few minutes of scrambling over tree roots and fallen branches, they saw the clearing up ahead. They had approached it from a different direction, but now they could see the Ford Capri exactly where it had been the previous evening. The driver's door still hung open, and as they got close to it they could see the keys still in the ignition.

Janie walked slowly around the car, looking for anything that might suggest what had happened when John's journey ended so abruptly.

'Ssh, did you hear that?' Libby said, grabbing Janie's arm.

There was the sound of something crushing over twigs, in the near distance at first, gradually coming closer. Then the sound of leaves being trodden and moments later, a figure approached from the clearing.

'Dear Lord, Will. You scared us,' Libby said. 'What are you doing here?'

'I thought I'd come back, see the place in the daylight. Looks as if you decided to do the same thing?'

'We've found nothing to explain what happened,' Janie said. 'So, we've all had a wasted journey.'

Here was a chance to question Will without the others listening in. But a moment later the opportunity vanished as they watched Will mount his bike and cycle off down the track.

'He's in a hurry all of a sudden, isn't he?' Janie said.

'Could be he was hoping to have the place to himself?'

No more than fifty yards down the woodland track Will braked, throwing his bike to one side, crouching at first, then kneeling.

'Now what's he doing?' Libby said.

As they peered through the dappled light of overhead trees in new leaf, they saw Will pick something up and stuff it into his pocket.

'Whatever it is, it's as if he expected to find it. He didn't seem surprised,' Janie said. 'Come on.' She stepped forward at pace, her intention to reach Will before he remounted his bike and cycled off.

'Hey, Will,' Libby called out. 'What's that you've found?'

He stood and turned towards them, appearing indecisive. Within a moment they were standing beside him.

Janie couldn't tell if there was a reluctance in the way he put his hand in his pocket. Then he drew his hand out, revealing the item he had secreted there.

'It's John's wallet,' he said.

'What makes you say that?' Janie asked.

He passed the brown leather wallet over to Janie. She turned it over a couple of times, inspecting it for any signs that might indicate how it came to be there, some distance from John's abandoned car.

'Look inside,' Will said.

Janie opened the wallet and passed it to Libby. Any money that might have been tucked into the back of the wallet was gone. It was empty, except for a small black-and-white photo that sat behind a cut out window on the inside flap.

'His wife?' Janie asked, as she took in the smiling image of a beautiful young woman, dark hair cut into a bob shape, framing her face, a marked dimple in both cheeks.

Will nodded, returned to his bike and without another word cycled off into the distance.

CHAPTER 6

ON THE DRIVE BACK to the university Janie took the opportunity to mull over her thoughts. When she agreed to join Libby for the weekend conference, she hadn't really considered the content of the debates. It was the idea of a few days away, a breathing space, which had convinced her to take up Libby's suggestion. She and Greg had been arguing for a while. No, in truth it was more of a series of heated discussions. He accused her of being constantly diverted from her role as wife and mother. She retaliated, saying she believed she had the potential to be so much more.

'Aren't we enough for you?' was Greg's plea.

'It's not a case of giving up one thing to make space for another,' she said. 'You don't get it, do you?'

Since her Aunt Jessica had returned from Europe she and Janie had enjoyed many conversations about Jessica's travels. The more Janie heard, the more she reflected on her own life.

'We've lived such a small life,' she told her husband. 'Come on, tell me. Where have we been? Even our honeymoon was spent no more than twenty miles from Tamarisk Bay.'

'What, so now you wished we'd flown off somewhere? Some package holiday to Lloret de Mar, where we sit on a beach, get burned to a cinder, and come home with a toy donkey as our souvenir? And what about your dad? I thought you didn't ever want to be too far away from him?'

Since Philip Chandler's accident had left him blind he had learned to live a full and independent life. Janie's mother had left soon after, announcing she was sorry, but she wasn't cut out to be a nursemaid. Philip retrained as a physiotherapist and was loved and admired by a host of grateful patients. And Charlie, one of a succession of guide dogs, was Philip's constant companion. Nevertheless, alongside her job looking after the mobile library, Janie called in most days to check on her dad, taking care of any paperwork, making sure the fridge was well stocked and the place was clean and tidy. It was a responsibility she took on wholeheartedly, one that gave her pleasure, but now Jessica was around Janie wasn't needed quite so regularly.

It was as if an opening had appeared in a previously impenetrable forest. A forest she was ready to explore and Libby's press cutting presented the perfect first step. The last year or two, since Zara's disappearance, Janie's relationship with her husband had swayed more than a little. If their marriage could be likened to a seesaw, what had been in balance when they first married, was now constantly shifting. Her love for Greg hadn't diminished. And his recent move into the building trade proved he had a real talent. His boss had often complimented him on the neatness of his brickwork and Janie could hear the pleasure in her husband's voice when he told her about it. She was proud of him.

But as time passed Janie could feel herself changing. She had learned new skills, discovering she had a talent for tracking down missing people; first Zara, then all she did to help Mr Furness, and more recently the trouble with Luigi. On each occasion she'd felt on an equal footing with Detective Sergeant Bright. Yes, he'd made it clear she could be an irritation, but she was pretty sure he admired her too.

And it was all the juggling, between Dad, the library, and her investigations, that made her feel alive. Then there was her role as a mum and a wife. At three months old Michelle was beginning to express her personality, each day there was something new to wonder at. Her daughter's first smile, gurgles sounding as if she was even now trying to form words. She was a joy. But it was as if there were different segments in Janie's brain, that needed different types of food. Her reading fed one part, conversations with her dad another. Each time she held her daughter close, or had a kiss from Greg when he came in from work, she felt comforted and secure. But she had become increasingly aware there were other parts of her mind she needed to feed. Listening to the passion in Clem's voice when she spoke about women's rights, hearing Alison talk of equality, the same pay for the same work done, had sparked something in Janie. She could imagine what it would be like to study here at the university, and now there was this new concept of an Open University. Her mind raced ahead, imagining where it could all lead. A change in career, perhaps. Or a career per se, something with a chance for progression, promotion. The library van was a special place, she loved chatting to her customers, helping them find just the right books for themselves and their families.

Since the birth of her daughter Janie had passed the day-to-day responsibility for the library van back to Phyllis Frobisher, Libby's grandmother. Phyllis had run the mobile library for several years following her retirement from teaching. Once Janie took over Phyllis remained as back up and now the roles were reversed, with Phyllis taking on the lion's share of the work and Janie calling in regularly to help. Phyllis was happy to continue with the arrangement until Michelle was six months old. Then Janie would be back in charge again, taking her daughter with her into work, on the days she wasn't with her great aunt Jessica. It was a good arrangement, nevertheless Janie was discovering there were new avenues to explore.

Here at the university Janie was surrounded by the potential for learning, filling her with a sense of the possible. Building work was continuing across the site. Becky had mentioned there was to be a new research centre, and a building to house ground-breaking development in educational technology. But it was the main university library Janie longed to investigate. It was closed for the Easter break, but Janie could imagine the shelves, laden with books on every subject. A place where she could happily lose herself for hours, days.

Yet, despite all that, there was an irony. She had come to the conference thinking it would give her space to think, away from all responsibilities. And now, in the midst of all her thoughts, she was presented with yet another mystery. Another missing person. On the face of it there was nothing unusual about a man who goes for an evening drive and has an accident. But if someone had picked up him, why leave the car keys behind?

Janie's past investigations had been sparked by others. Hugh Furness had asked for her help, and Luigi was a troubled soul who had created concerns for her aunt and her dad. It was only the search for Zara she had instigated. On that occasion her dad told her to trust her instincts, and her earlier phone call to him that morning suggested she do the same.

What were her instincts telling her? Will had discovered John's wallet empty of money. Had someone run him off the road, then robbed him? It seemed like a lot of trouble to go to for the sake of a few pounds. Even if the wallet was stuffed full of money, how would the assailant have known that? Unless the person Olivia had seen arguing with John had known about the money and followed him?

The police would undertake a thorough search of the area. Something she and Libby weren't in a position to do effectively. Will had picked up the wallet before Janie could tell him not to. From all she had learned about police investigations, she knew they would want to know precisely where the wallet had been found, they would probably check fingerprints too. And now Will's fingerprints were all over the wallet and hers too.

Then there were the unanswered questions surrounding the relationship between Will and John. He clearly recognised the picture of John's wife. Was there unfinished business between Will and John?

And the phone call from John's wife. Was there more to the message? If Janie could speak to Peter, the young man who had taken the phone call from Mrs Bramber, it might provide a slim thread that could, in turn, lead her to an unravelling.

CHAPTER 7

MOST OF THE USUAL term-time complement of university kitchen staff had taken the opportunity of the Easter break to enjoy a holiday. All except Marjorie Blackmore. So determined was Marjorie not to hand over responsibility for her beloved kitchen that she hadn't taken a proper holiday since the university first opened some nine years earlier. She had learned her lesson some years back when she returned from a day off to attend a family funeral to find the salt pot had been moved from its usual place beside the row of ovens. She found it eventually, sitting on a shelf next to granulated sugar. She never did identify the culprit as no one was owning up. But she vowed there and then that it would be her last day off.

'I'll be here until the day I retire,' she announced to the Vice Chancellor. 'Unless they carry me out in a box first.'

All the Vice Chancellor could feel was a sense of relief as he had been told by staff and students alike that Marjorie Blackmore was irreplaceable.

And so the call went out for a temporary kitchen helper. Peter heard about the job by chance through a friend of a friend. Since leaving the children's home he had yet to find a full-time job. Some weeks he'd had two or three jobs on the go, while for several days in-between there was no chance of earning a single penny.

His rent for the house share his social worker had helped to organise took most of any wages he could cobble together, so he always looked for jobs in cafes, bars, or kitchens. One meal a day was always included as a benefit, which meant he didn't have to worry about buying food. Except for the days he wasn't working, days when he often survived on a pie from the local bakers, eating it cold to save putting money into the electricity meter.

'They'll be wanting their lunch at one o'clock, so we need to have it ready at least ten minutes before that,' was Marjorie's instruction earlier that morning to Peter.

Since his seven 'o'clock start Peter had switched happily from preparing the vegetables for this evening's supper to clearing away the dishes from the visitors' breakfast. Washing up was down to him too, something he was more than used to from his time in the children's home. In Claremont Mount the older children were given a choice of weekend chores; shoe cleaning, sweeping the floors, or helping out in the kitchen. The helping out invariably involved washing or drying the dishes, which he found preferable to any of the other tasks by a long way. Today there was another reminder of those days, when Marjorie told him corned beef hash was on the supper menu for the delegates. Peter could still conjure up the taste of his favourite meal of the week, his plate always liberally splattered with tomato sauce. The cook at Claremont Mount managed to get a really crispy top on the hash, which the children always fought over. The best of all was a corner piece, with the odd piece of burnt onion sticking out, waiting to be picked up and crunched as if it was a potato crisp.

'And you passed the message on this morning, did you?' Marjorie was busy putting the finishing touches to the leek and potato soup, tasting it for salt.

'I told the organiser. Clem Richmond is it? It was only by chance I was there by the phone when it rang.'

'And you say it was someone's wife?'

'A Mrs Bramber. But when I told Miss Richmond, she looked quite surprised.'

'You did the right thing, and remember, whatever is going on out there is none of our business.' Marjorie waved her hand in the direction of the outer corridor.

'The notices say they're here to talk about women's rights and all that stuff. But there were several men amongst the delegates at supper last night. They must feel pretty outnumbered, mustn't they? I know I would.'

'We just keep them fed and watered and mind our own business. But if you want my opinion, I can't see what all the fuss is about. I like being a woman and I definitely don't fancy being a man. We each have our own strengths without having to fight about it. After all, men can't give birth, can they?' Her laugh was more of a cackle, soon followed by a chesty cough. 'Pass me that pan, there's a love, then start taking the bread from the wrappers and laying it out on those plates.'

For a while they worked side-by-side in silence, Marjorie occasionally humming a tune, which Peter didn't recognise. It was only the second day he had worked alongside Marjorie, but he already wished more than anything he didn't have to leave once the weekend was over. Come Monday, it would be back into the same round of knocking on doors, looking for work.

When he told his friend he'd been accepted for the job Peter had joked. 'I'll be able to tell everyone I've been to university.' But after the joke he thought more about the possibilities that studying might offer him. Not at university; that would really be beyond him. But there were college courses where he could learn the catering trade. Having a piece of paper to say he knew how to do things properly was bound to make it easier to get a permanent place, to make a career of it. Trouble was how would he ever afford it? If he had to go to college five days a week he wouldn't be able to work enough hours to earn enough to pay the rent. It was hopeless. He thumped the last slice of bread onto the remainder of the pile.

'Hey there, what's up with you?' Marjorie said.

'Sorry, Mrs Blackmore. I didn't mean to...'

'I can see from your face you're all riled up. What is it, lad? Do you want to talk about it?'

'It's fine, really. I'll get the stuff ready to take out to the counter, shall I?'

'Why not take a minute, eh? Step outside; the fresh air will do you good.'

The yard at the back of the canteen offered little by way of fresh air, rather an overriding smell from the rubbish bins and the pig bin. Peter sat on an upturned milk crate, filled a cigarette paper with a sliver of tobacco, licked the paper to seal the edges, then lit it. He took a long drag, watching the cigarette smoke waft upwards in spirals. He was thirteen when he first shared a cigarette with Billy Townsend, another of the boys in the children's home. Billy was a couple of years older and never seemed to mind when the younger boys followed him around. Billy always had a cigarette to share, and it was clear Billy saw it as some sort of kudos, as if he was admired for something other than his ability to snatch not only cigarettes, from the local shop, but often chocolate too.

A rumour spread after Billy left the children's home that he was caught for something far worse than a bit of shoplifting. The word was he moved on to housebreaking, tried his luck once too often and was now doing a prison stretch.

A nearby sound made him turn to see a woman approaching.

'Hello there. Sorry, I'm interrupting your break.'

The woman had a woollen scarf wrapped around her shoulders, over the top of her coat. Peter was still in his shirt sleeves and looking at the woman he was suddenly conscious a brisk wind was funnelling through the yard, making him shiver.

'I need to get back, it's nearly time to serve lunch. I've only been allowed out for a quick ciggie.'

'You work in the kitchen, do you?'

Peter nodded, briefly wondering why the woman had ventured into the yard, which was not on a route from or to any other part of the campus.

'I'm Mrs Juke, by the way. Janie.' She held out a hand towards Peter, who was unsure whether to shake it.

'Peter Rowland,' he said, standing and moving towards the door, anxious to escape to the relative safety of the kitchen.

'Ah, Peter. And you're the student who's helping to prepare our meals. Well, we're really grateful you've given up your holiday to be here.'

There was too much to explain and no need to tell this woman anything about his personal circumstances, so he remained silent.

'Do you mind if I ask you something before you go?' Janie said.

He shrugged and waited.

'You took a phone call this morning? From a Mrs Bramber, is that right?'

He shrugged again.

'It's just that we're not too sure where Mr Bramber is. He was one of our group, but no one has seen him since yesterday, since before last night's supper. There was a thought that he could have gone home, but that phone call you took confirmed that isn't the case. Do you mind telling me exactly what Mrs Bramber said?'

As Peter listened, he was forming a question of his own.

'What's it to you?' he said.

'It seems a bit strange, that's all. Someone's there one minute and the next, well...plus we found his car abandoned in the woods near here.'

'How come you're the one asking about him?'

'Between you and me, I've got some experience in tracking down missing people.'

'You're with the police?'

Janie shook her head and gave a little laugh. 'No, nothing like that. I'm a librarian.'

'Seems like a funny thing, a librarian looking for missing people.'

'It's something I kind of stumbled into,' Janie said.

'Are you good at it?' Peter had stepped away from the door and was studying Janie's face as if it would provide him with the answer to his question.

'Pretty good, yes. Why?'

'I might be looking for someone myself. And if I am, but if that someone doesn't want to be found, I don't stand a chance, do I?' He didn't wait for Janie's reply, as moments later he was back in the kitchen, loading cutlery onto a tray, with Marjorie still humming in the background.

CHAPTER 8

LUNCH WAS ALREADY UNDERWAY when Libby entered the refectory. A hint of onion-flavoured steam wafted across the room. Most of the delegates had already been up to the serving counter, returning to their tables to continue fervent conversations.

Bryony, Olivia, Alison, and Clem were in the same seats they had taken at breakfast. Libby plumped herself down on her chair, glancing dismally at the empty chair beside her. John's empty chair.

Libby had just returned to her seat, carefully negotiating a full bowl of soup and a couple of slices of bread, hoping to avoid any mishap. Then Will came in, still sweating from his cycle ride. He gave a sideways glance at Libby before sitting.

'Where's Janie?' Alison asked.

'She'll be here in a second,' Libby said, just as Janie came in through the double doors behind her.

'Will found this in the woods, not far from John's car,' Janie said, placing the wallet beside Clem's soup plate.

For a while, all that could be heard was the clattering of spoons and soup bowls as the other delegates who had finished eating gathered up their crockery.

'Is it John's?' Clem said, picking up the wallet and opening it.

'Yep, it's his alright,' Will said.

'No money?' Olivia was next to speak, straining to see the wallet, but remaining in her seat.

'If there was money in it, it's gone now. Whoever took John took his money too. At least that's what I reckon,' Will said.

'You think someone has taken him?' Libby said. 'But why would anyone do that? Steal his money, yes, I can see that. But abducting someone? What on earth would be the motive?'

'Right, it's more than twelve hours since anyone has seen John. We've found his car abandoned, and now his empty wallet. So, I'll not delay any further. I'm ringing the police right now.' Janie's words were calm but firm. 'I've dealt with the police before, I'm happy to speak to them and trust me, they aren't going to be worried about the rights and wrongs of women campaigning for equal rights. Their focus will be on finding John, which is what ours should be.'

Janie took her seat beside Libby, who patted her on the back. 'Well said, I couldn't have put it better myself. Clem, you mentioned you've had a run in with the police. You weren't arrested, were you?'

Clem pushed her plate of unfinished soup away and stood. She lit a cigarette, as if those few moments would give her a chance to prepare her thoughts.

'Nothing like that, but I've spent the last two years studying here at Sussex and I've read enough to know that the underdog is always pilloried, accused of wrongdoings, often without evidence.'

'Do you study criminal law?' Janie asked.

Clem shook her head. 'English literature. But it's all there in the classical texts. They prove time and again the establishment want nothing more than to control. If it's not women who end up suffering, it's the working classes. You've only to go back to before the industrial revolution. Look at the way tenant farmers were treated by wealthy landowners.'

'I can't see what any of that has to do with bringing in the police to deal with a potential crime. Unless you feel guilty about something. Is that it, Clem? Are you worried you're going to be found out?' Janie said.

Alison slammed her hand down on the table, an action so out of character it gained everyone's attention. 'Clem might have strong views, but she is not a criminal. You can trust me on that one.'

'You said you were at school together?' Libby asked.

Alison gave the slightest nod. 'John would vouch for her too if he was here.'

Will had wandered away from the table. Now he turned towards Alison as if to say something, but remained silent.

'Is that right, Will? You and John know Clem from school days?' Janie asked. 'And you recognised that photo of John's wife, didn't you? What are you not telling us, Will?'

The question didn't go unnoticed by Clem, who glared at Janie and Libby. 'It's you two who are the strangers here.'

'You all know each other? Bryony, Olivia? Why go through that farce yesterday with those introductions? Was it just for our benefit?' Libby said.

It seemed any remaining soup would be returned to the kitchen untouched. Clem finished one cigarette and immediately lit another, tipping the ash into an ashtray that Alison held as she stood beside her.

Janie chose the moment to take charge. 'Clem, I think you should alert your colleagues. They should know that one of our group is missing. It will be worth checking with the rest of the delegates. There's a chance someone might have seen something or someone that might be relevant. Meanwhile I'll just explain to the police what we know and what we don't know. They'll send someone over pretty soon, I'm sure, and they'll want to talk to each of us. So my advice is don't go far, stay on campus at least.'

And with that Janie was gone, leaving Libby to hear the backlash.

'Who does she think she is?' Olivia's indignance was evident. 'Telling us what we should do and where we should be. I'll not be told what to do by anyone, certainly not by the likes of her. She's only a librarian, for goodness sake.'

'And what's that supposed to mean?' Libby said, coming to the defence of her friend.

'Stop it, just stop it, all of you.' To hear Bryony's voice at such a loud pitch brought the others to silence once more. 'If you're all going to argue, I'm out of here.' She took the bag from the back of her chair and ran out.

'She's a liability, that woman,' Olivia said, aiming her words at Clem. 'I can't think why you invited her.'

'I didn't invite her. She got in touch a week ago, asking if there was space for her to come along,' Clem replied.

'Do you know what?' Libby pulled a chair over from the table and sat down. 'I think it's about time we had some honesty. If you know more about John than you've said until now, what is it you're hiding? Because from where I'm standing not one of you has been very forthcoming.'

'You love to ask questions, don't you? Clem said. 'Makes me think you must be a reporter. You didn't exactly give much away when you introduced yourself. "Writing words" could mean just about anything, but that's it, isn't it? You're here to grab a scoop about women overturning the world order? You know it's people like you who give us students a bad name. It's all there in the latest uni magazine. You reporters are just looking for trouble, hoping to grab the best headline. Television is doing the self-same thing, poking their cameras into people's faces, making a mockery of what we're trying to achieve. This isn't some fictional drama offered for the entertainment of the masses, this is real life. Thousands of us are being ignored, suffering injustice, stripped of any real chance of achievement, just because we're female. And you're here to grab a story, a front page exclusive, which I'm guessing will help your career no end. And as a woman, you should be ashamed of yourself.'

Clem drew a breath, her cheeks fiery red with indignation.

'My oh my. Quite a speech there, Clem. Yes, I'm a reporter, but only on a local paper. I'm here on my own time because I'm genuinely interested in all the things you're planning to discuss. My editor doesn't even know I'm here. And yes, Janie and I are concerned about John's disappearance, but you must be too.'

'Looks to me as if you're more than just a little concerned about John,' Will said. 'You were getting awfully pally with him yesterday, considering you'd never met him before and considering John is a married man.'

'Look, there's no real mystery to it,' Alison said, clearly hoping to calm the rising tension. 'Clem, Olivia, and I know each other from school. We lost track of each other when school ended. Then Clem and I met up again. It's like I told you. She and I took part in a couple of protest marches.'

'And Bryony?' Libby asked.

'Bryony, yes. We all stayed on to do A Levels, but she didn't...' Olivia's voice tailed off, as though she had said more than she intended.

'Bryony's not like us,' Clem said. 'I mean, she's had a few problems.'

'So much for female solidarity,' Libby said. 'From where I'm standing it sounds as though Bryony could have benefitted from the hand of friendship and what she got instead was prejudice and snobbery.'

'I resent that,' Olivia stamped her foot.

'Resent all you like. But listen to yourselves.' Libby turned to Will who was the only one to have remained standing by the window, his back to the others. 'And John? Where does he fit into all of this?'

Will was saved from answering as Olivia stepped in. 'My husband and John are involved in business together.'

'What sort of business?' Libby said.

'I've no idea. My husband and I don't discuss work, we never have done.'

'Come on, what's the big secret you're all trying to hide?' Libby asked.

'Why should we tell you anything?' Will turned towards Libby. 'Clem's right, if it's a negative story you're after then you need to look elsewhere.'

'You're wrong about me. But I'll tell you what, if I decided to write an article, I'd have plenty to write about, wouldn't I? Let's take you, Will. A self-declared hippy, who's been living in a commune. Escaping real life, are you? Some dark past? Then there's Clem, angry enough about men in general it seems, to blame them for all the things that are wrong in your life. What's the truth, Clem? Have you been let down by a man? Had your heart broken? And Olivia. Why would you leave your rich, comfortable life to come and sit in a freezing room and discuss equal pay for women, when it's pretty clear to me you've never had a real job in your life? And poor Bryony. Scared of her own shadow. You say you know her and yet not one of you has reached out to make her feel included.'

'The knives are really out, aren't they?' Clem said. 'You're the perfect example of the kind of reporter who enjoys printing lies about honest, ordinary people just to help sell more newspapers.'

'Yeah, well you know what they say about truth, it hurts, doesn't it, Clem?' Libby said, slamming the door behind her.

CHAPTER 9

LIBBY STOOD OUTSIDE FALMER House hoping the chilling breeze would cool her flushed cheeks. She had said more than she'd intended, passing judgement on people she barely knew. She felt particularly bad about her verbal attack on Will. He had chosen a different way of life, nothing wrong with that. In some ways Will made Libby think of her dad, who she had met for the first time when she was three years old. Later, when she was older, she discovered he had had what some might describe as a chequered past. He was in her life for a short time before heading off to Greece. Over the ensuing years she had the occasional letter from him, but knew very little about how he led his life out there. Perhaps he was in one of the communes that Will had described. More than anything Libby hoped he was happy. She still dreamed that one day she would turn up and surprise him. His little Primrose all grown up.

Now, feeling embarrassed about her outburst, she was grateful at the thought that the police would soon arrive to take control, leaving her and Janie to be nothing more than interested bystanders. The truth was that helping Janie to solve past mysteries had given Libby a taste for the intrigue, seeking clues, gathering evidence, analysing motives. Despite herself she reflected on what she had blurted out earlier. Of all of them it seemed Bryony was the most innocent. Yet she knew from experience it was often the quiet, seemingly innocent people who had the most to hide. Bryony had run out of the dining room. Perhaps this was the moment to follow her, catch her on her own and ask her a few pertinent questions to discover if she really was as shy and innocent as she appeared to be.

She spotted Bryony in the distance on the far side of the car park. There was no mistaking her as she was still wearing the denim jacket she had worn since her arrival on campus. She had even worn it during last night's supper. Yes, the classroom was cold, but the refectory hardly warranted a coat to be worn. The evening before Bryony said she had seen John driving off. Could it be that having a cigarette wasn't the only reason for her being out there?

As Libby walked towards the car park, she watched Bryony get into a pale blue Austin. Bryony had given the impression she had little money, and yet it seemed she had enough to own and run a car? Admittedly, the car had more rust on it than paintwork and was likely even older than Libby's Mini, so it wasn't such a stretch to think Bryony could afford it.

Libby watched Bryony pull away before slipping into her own car and setting off in pursuit. Bryony's old Austin proceeded slowly enough, a relief to Libby who would never have been able to cope with a fast speed. She smiled to herself as she thought of what Janie would say. Something along the lines that Libby was the least likely driver to mount a car chase.

The Austin headed north, taking the same road Janie and Libby had taken earlier that day. Bryony continued past the clearing where John's car was still standing abandoned, over a narrow bridge and down a dip towards more open countryside. If Bryony had noticed she was being followed she gave no indication of slowing or altering her route, which was steadily northwards. After five minutes or so, the Austin began to increase its speed with Libby gripping tighter to her steering wheel as she determined to keep pace. The road led on into the South Downs, with several hairpin bends to negotiate.

As the morning morphed into afternoon, it was as though the sun couldn't make up its mind. One minute it was tucked behind a wispy cloud, the next choosing to shine brightly, catching Libby through the side window, make it difficult for her to concentrate on the road ahead. She was cursing herself that she had never bothered to fix the broken sun visor. If it wasn't hanging off its one remaining fixing she might have been able to twist it to the side to block out the blinding rays that kept catching at her line of sight.

She took one of the sharp bends too haphazardly at the same moment a farm vehicle came towards her. Libby held her breath, manoeuvring to the far left-hand side of the road, certain she would end up in the ditch that ran alongside. With the farm truck safely past, Libby focused again on the Austin up ahead, its speed still increasing. She watched as Bryony's car reached the top of an ascent, only to disappear down the other side. Before Libby gained sight of the downward side of the hill, she heard a dreadful screech, metal on metal, followed instantly by an almighty thud. Libby had the Austin in full view. The car lay on its side, smoke billowing from the engine. She brought her own car to a stop a few yards behind the Austin and ran towards it.

'Bryony,' she screamed.

As Libby stood beside the car, she had Bryony in clear view. The young woman was slumped sideways, partly onto the passenger seat, her head thrown back from the force of the crash, a stream of blood running across the collar of her jacket.

'Oh no, dear God. Bryony, can you hear me? Please say something.'

Libby tugged at the driver's door, which appeared to be jammed closed. At the same time she was aware of the continuous stream of smoke coming from the engine. From her work as a reporter, she knew enough about car crashes to know that one of the biggest dangers was leaking petrol, which could easily be ignited by the heat from the engine. Once that happened, if that happened, the car would explode and there would be zero chance of getting Bryony out alive. That's even if she was still alive. As things were at this moment Libby couldn't tell either way. Her only chance was somehow to force open the driver's door and drag Bryony out. She had moments only, no time to think, no time to plan.

She ran back to her car, threw open the boot and feverishly rifled through the mix of rubbish that filled it. An old coat, a pair of wellingtons, two handbags she had meant to throw out but couldn't bring herself to. A picnic rug was pushed up into one corner of the boot and under the rug were a few tools she'd been told she would need if she ever got a puncture. Even when she put the tools into the car, she vowed she would never use them. *If I get a puncture, I'll be hailing down the nearest man to fix it for me.* Her brief thought now was, *So much for equality, Libby,* as she threw a thank you prayer up to the heavens. *Whoever suggested I might need these is now my very favourite person.*

The wheel brace had no sharp end. She would need something thin to prise the driver's door open. She could try to smash the window, but that would send glass flying all over Bryony and might still not help to open the door. Jammed up in the far corner of the boot was a spanner. *That might just work.*

As she stepped close to the Austin once more, the smoke coming from the engine was becoming increasingly dense and there was a strong smell of petrol. Libby forced the spanner into the narrow gap between the edge of the driver's door and the main bodywork. She pushed it firmly forward and yet all it did was slip out again.

Come on, Libby. What's all that keep fit for if you can't even summon up the strength to open a door?

She held her breath and tightened every muscle she could, then thrust the spanner into the gap once more. This time something seemed to give way. She tried the handle again, tugging on it, all the time willing Bryony to make a movement, any movement to show she was still alive.

'Bryony, please, please. Can you hear me? I'm going to get you out, I promise. But I really need your help.'

With no response coming from inside the car, all Libby could do was pull on the handle again, this time putting her foot against the body of the car to give her more leverage. Moments later her efforts proved successful, the door flying open, throwing Libby backwards, landing heavily on the road surface. There was no time to worry about any cuts or scrapes, as she scrambled to her feet, able to reach Bryony for the first time since the Austin had sped out of control.

Libby lent into the car laying her hands gently on Bryony's side, her tone calm as she tried to establish if Bryony was conscious. And then, after what seemed like hours since the crash, but in truth was barely minutes, Libby felt Bryony move. The movement was so minimal Libby wondered if she had imagined it. But no, Bryony was conscious and straining to lift herself from her prone position.

'Easy now,' Libby said. 'Let me help you. We need to get you out of here but it's important we do it gently. Can you move your legs?'

A small nod from Bryony reassured Libby that there was a chance.

'We'll do it together, lean on me as much as you like.'

As Libby encouraged and Bryony tested first her legs, then her arms, between them they managed to slide her over closer to the open driver's door. The rusty door hinges were a blessing, making it easy for Libby to force the door back on itself. The opening was wide enough to ease Bryony out. Blood trickling down the side of Bryony's face was coming from a wide gash on her forehead; working out what other injuries she might have suffered could wait until she had moved Bryony well clear of potential danger.

'I don't understand what happened, I had my foot hard down on the brake, but the car kept going faster and faster.' Bryony's words were broken by heavy gasps as pain and shock took hold.

They sat together on a grassy area beside the road, watching smoke still billowing from the engine.

'Where does it hurt? Is anything broken?' Libby took Bryony's hand in hers, hoping to infuse her with reassurance.

'I don't know, I don't think so. But my head, it hurts so much.'

There was a noticeable slurring to Bryony's words, making Libby even more anxious. She couldn't leave her to call for help. Bryony might collapse at any moment from concussion, or worse.

'I'm going to try to get you into my car. Can you manage that? We need to get you to hospital.'

'I'm not sure I can move. Can't you ring for an ambulance?'

'I have no idea how far the nearest phone box is and right now there's no way I'm going to leave you.'

It was only now Libby realised she hadn't seen a single car pass them. Since the moment of the crash they had been alone on that stretch of road. And then, as if conjured up purely by wishful thinking, she heard the sound of a motorbike approaching and watched it slow and then come to a stop. The rider put his bike on its stand, removed his crash helmet, and ran over to where Libby and Bryony were sitting.

'You alright there? That looks nasty.'

'My friend needs to go to hospital, but I can't leave her. Could you ring for an ambulance?'

It was only much later that Libby realised she hadn't noticed anything about the man's face, not even noting his age. She remembered his black leathers, the metal studs across both shoulders, but little else.

The man hesitated for a second or two, before donning his helmet once again, returning to his bike and speeding off in the direction he had come from.

'Help will be here soon, I promise,' Libby said, acknowledging to herself that it wasn't only Bryony who needed assistance. If the motorbike rider hadn't turned up at that moment Libby had no idea what she would have done. Her hands were shaking uncontrollably. In fact, she wasn't sure if she could ever sit behind a steering wheel again.

CHAPTER 10

WHEN JANIE RETURNED FROM having phoned the police her first thoughts were to talk to Libby and between them to formulate a plan. She knew from her previous dealings with the police in Tamarisk Bay that once they were involved, they would want to take charge. It made sense. After all, they had the necessary experience in evidence gathering, in questioning techniques, and in building a case once a criminal had been identified. But Janie and Libby had their own approach, one that might be just as valid. Often people were loath to speak to the police for one reason or another. Clem's antipathy towards the police was a case in point. Through gentle persuasion and a focus on listening, rather than interrogation, Janie had frequently found she encouraged people to open up.

A good place to start would be to explore the connections between Clem's discussion group. They knew each other, and they knew John, and yet they seemed reticent to share that information with her or with Libby.

Clem and Alison were sitting on a wall outside Falmer House when Janie approached. They were deep in conversation, but stopped talking as soon as they saw her. Clem was balancing an open cigarette packet on her knee, seemingly intrigued to see if it would remain there once she let go of it.

The friendship between the two of them was an interesting one. Clem was fiery, passionate about the causes she believed in. Alison was more measured in her opinions and behaviour. And yet there was an underlying strength in Alison that Clem seemed to rely on. Perhaps Alison's steadying nature had helped Clem through difficult times. Clem said she was two years into her degree, meaning she wouldn't have started it until she was twenty-one, some three years after completing her A-levels. What had she been doing during those three years? Had she failed in a chosen career, only to return to university to bolster her confidence? Perhaps her outspoken views had got her into trouble, resulting in her being sacked, or worse still ending in a run-in with the law.

But at that moment Janie's focus was on speaking to Libby to share all the ideas that were buzzing round her mind.

'Is Libby inside?' she asked.

'What did the police have to say?' Clem said, still focused on the cigarette packet. 'You wait, they'll arrive just in time to see John walking back in, wondering what all the fuss is about.'

'They're sending someone over. They'll want to speak to everyone. Has Libby gone back to Park Village?'

'She went off in her car.' It was Will who answered, coming up behind Janie and nodding towards the car park.

'Did she say where she was going?'

'She'll be on the phone to her editor, I bet,' Clem said. 'Probably hoping to score points for some pathetic scoop or other. Trust me, reporters are all the same, taking pleasure in other people's misery.'

'That doesn't even deserve a response,' Janie said, walking away and towards Park Village.

'She doesn't mean it, you know.' Will was a step behind Janie, catching up level with her as she pulled the door open to the student digs. 'When she feels threatened, she hits out. She would have had such grand hopes for this weekend, thinking it would make a mark, hoping it would get her recognised as someone who can achieve change. Now she sees it all going wrong. She'll probably apologise later.'

'It's Libby she needs to apologise to.' Janie continued up the stairs to the first floor and along the corridor towards her bedroom, with

Will still behind her. 'What do you want, Will?' She held the door handle, keeping the door closed, waiting for Will to speak.

'Can we talk?'

Without replying, Janie pushed open the bedroom door, hoping she would find Libby inside. Instead the room was empty.

'Why would she have driven off like that? You're sure she didn't leave a message for me?'

Will hovered in the doorway, appearing uncertain about whether to step into the room. 'She didn't say anything to me, maybe she spoke to one of the others?'

'Can this wait, Will? The police will be here any minute and I'd prefer to be around when they get here. Otherwise Clem is bound to tell them they're not needed and we'll be no further forward.'

Will stepped forward, his expression set as if he had reached a decision. 'I want to explain about John and me. You asked me how it was that I recognised that photo of John's wife. Well, you're right, we do have history. The thing is we were both in love with the same girl and she chose John. That's it, really. No big deal.'

It was clear to Janie from Will's tone and his sullen expression that it was far from 'no big deal'.

'How long have they been married?'

'A few years.'

'And you knew John would be here this weekend? You've stayed in touch?'

'I've been abroad. Spent a while travelling the Greek islands, trying to get over my broken heart.'

'And did you? Get over it, I mean?'

Will shrugged and turned to walk away. 'You'll want to get downstairs, in case the police arrive. But Janie, I'd appreciate it if you didn't say anything to the police about my knowing John, they might think I'd be happy to have him out of the way to leave the coast clear for me and Helena.'

'And is that your agenda? Did you and Helena plan it between you?'

Will was at the far end of the landing, speaking without turning to look at Janie, who had come to stand in the doorway. 'You've read too many books, Janie, you're imagining some awful conspiracy where there is none.'

Watching him go down the staircase Janie reflected on Will's accusation. Perhaps she was seeing some mysterious chain of events, when the truth was far more straightforward.

Grabbing her scarf from the end of the bed she pulled the door closed and headed downstairs and out towards Falmer House. Clem and Alison were sitting in the same place they had been in earlier, now joined by Olivia, who waved at Janie as she approached.

'Cooee, there you are. What did the police say?'

Janie couldn't help but be irritated at Olivia's manner. She seemed to be treating the whole thing as nothing more than a 'jolly jape'.

'They'll be here soon. They'll want to talk to you, all of us in fact. They'll try to establish if we know where John might have been going, what might have happened to him. It's important you tell them about the argument you saw, Olivia.'

'That? Oh, I could have been mistaken. I wouldn't want to mislead them with something and nothing. Like I said, I didn't hear what was being discussed. I couldn't even give a description of the other person.'

'Anything you saw will be useful, often it's the smallest clue that can lead to solving a crime.'

'A crime, you say?' Olivia said. 'So you're sure there's been a crime? You seem to know an awful lot about it.'

There was no time to respond, no time to explain, because at that moment Libby came running towards Janie, her arms scratched and bleeding and the front of her jacket spattered with blood.

'Oh, Janie. The most terrible thing has happened. It's Bryony, she's on her way to hospital, she's been badly hurt. It was truly awful, I thought she was dead.'

CHAPTER II

LIBBY HAD NO REAL recollection of her return journey. She had waited for the ambulance to arrive, watched as the ambulance men guided Bryony into the back of the ambulance, and remembered to check which hospital she was being taken to.

'I'll fetch Janie and we'll be right there with you. I promise you won't be on your own,' she told Bryony.

Watching Bryony's car careering over the brow of the hill, knowing before it happened, that the Austin would crash; and that the crash would result in Bryony losing her life, was a horror Libby would replay for a long time to come. It was the feeling of powerlessness that was so terrifying. Seconds felt like minutes. All she could do was watch it happen.

Afterwards she had to get into her own car and drive. She had no choice, although for a moment she considered the idea of sitting on the side of the road until someone – anyone – came to find her. Eventually she got into the driving seat, put the key into the ignition, and started the engine. All the way back she barely got out of second gear.

It was only when she saw Janie that the full force of the shock hit her and all she could do was to let the tears fall as Janie held her close and told her to take deep breaths.

'Take it slowly, you've had a terrible shock. Come inside and we'll get you a hot drink with plenty of sugar.'

The others followed Janie and Libby in through the swing doors and on into the refectory. Once inside Janie made Libby sit while the others stood around her, appearing almost as shocked as she was, but for the moment remaining silent.

'Give her some air, will you?' Janie waved her arms at them, at which point they all moved away a little, their focus still on Libby.

'I'll fetch her a cup of tea, shall I?' Alison said, not waiting for an answer before disappearing into the kitchen.

'Where were you going?' Clem said. 'Were you following Bryony? Is that why you saw her crash?'

'Leave her be, Clem.' Janie moved to shield Libby by standing in front of her.

'I'm just saying it's quite a coincidence, isn't it? The reporter is the one who makes sure she's "at the scene" on hand to gather all the gory details.'

'What is wrong with you?' Janie said. 'Can't you see Libby's really shaken up. And what about Bryony, doesn't anyone care how she is?'

'Janie, we need to go to the hospital. I promised Bryony we'd be there with her. But I can't drive us, I don't think I'll ever be able to drive again.' Libby had found her voice, but it was barely a whisper.

'There's time for that. Right now, I need you to drink this tea while it's hot.' Alison arrived with a mug of tea, which she put on the table beside Libby. 'Come on now, take a few sips.'

As Libby moved forward to pick up the mug it was as if she had only just noticed the cuts and grazes on her hands and arms. Splashes of dried blood stained the front of her jacket as well as her skirt.

The jacket was surely ruined. She remembered the day she dragged Janie along to the shop window where the jacket was on display. It was weeks of saving up before the day Libby was able to go into the shop, try it on and buy it. Janie was with her that day too, along with Michelle who seemed to have an unaccountable fascination for the large black buttons that finished off the jacket. Classic Biba in style, the black and white houndstooth design, with its wide lapels and nipped-in waist, fitted Libby like a glove.

'Stunning,' Janie had told her friend as she strutted proudly around the shop, feeling as if she had won the pools.

Now the stylish jacket was splashed with the blood of a young woman who may be fighting for her life.

Janie was speaking, bringing Libby back to the present. 'Let's get those cuts cleaned, we don't want them getting infected, do we?' Janie turned to Clem. 'Where's the first aid stuff?'

'Who's in charge here?'

The sharp voice caused them all to turn. In the doorway of the refectory stood a tall, thin-faced man, his suit jacket a perfect fit over broad shoulders. Beside him stood a young female officer in uniform, large horn-rimmed glasses disguising any other facial features.

'Detective Inspector Cooper, Sussex Constabulary,' the man said. 'We've had notification of a missing person. A Mr John Bramber.'

The sudden presence of the two police officers appeared to render the group speechless for several moments.

And then Janie explained. 'I rang the station, officer.'

'And you are?'

'Mrs Janie Juke.'

'And you're the organiser of this...' His voice tailed off. Before he could complete his sentence Clem stood, offering her hand out to shake his.

'Clem Richmond. I'm the organiser of this debating weekend on the subject of women's rights.'

Although she held her hand out to the senior officer, her focus was on the young policewoman, as though she somehow found her wanting.

'Mrs Richmond,' the detective said, 'we need to ask you all a few questions.'

'Miss. I haven't accepted the yoke of marriage. I'm my own person and not prepared to be dictated to by any man.' Clem's tone was as forceful as her words.

'That's all well and good, Miss. But I'm not here to join in your debate. My job here is to determine if Mr John Bramber is indeed missing, or if he's chosen to have a gadabout somewhere. So I'll need as much as information as you can provide, timing, circumstances and so on. Mrs Juke, you reported the incident, perhaps you could run through it again with my constable here. She'll take down the particulars. I'm assuming someone has spoken to Mr Bramber's wife? Or perhaps he has chosen not to take on the yoke of marriage?' A courteous smile in Clem's direction was met with a surly glare.

'And who is responsible for the delay in reporting this man missing?' Cooper continued. 'As I understand it, he hasn't been seen since yesterday evening. His car was found abandoned in the woods, and yet it's only now the police have been notified. Precious hours have been wasted. Hours that might mean the difference between finding Mr Bramber safe and well and a variety of alternatives.' Cooper scanned the faces of the group, not directing his comments at any one person. Then Will intervened.

'Detective Inspector Cooper, I'm Will Torrance and I wonder if you'd let me contact Mrs Bramber in the first instance. You see she doesn't know her husband is missing. As far as she's concerned he's here for the weekend debate.'

'And you know that because...?'

'Mrs Bramber rang here this morning. She wanted us to pass a message on to her husband. So you see, sir, the fact that he's missing, it would come as a shock to her.'

The detective looked Will up and down, taking in his bare feet, worn leather sandals and cheesecloth shirt, before his gaze moved to Libby. Until this moment the others had inadvertently formed a protective wall around her. With their focus on the new police presence, Libby's recent trauma had been momentarily forgotten.

'What's happened here then, eh?' the detective said.

'I was about to tell you, Detective Inspector. Libby has just witnessed a terrible accident. Bryony, she's another of our debating group; her car crashed north of here and right now she's on her way to hospital,' Janie said.

'I see,' the detective said. 'Williams, perhaps you could speak to Miss Libby...'

'Frobisher,' Janie said. 'Miss Libby Frobisher.'

'Yes, well, she looks pretty shaken up to me. So a woman's touch won't go amiss. Or do you consider that inappropriate? Not in line with your egalitarian attitudes?' His questions were directed at Clem who chose to turn her back to him.

The policewoman crouched down beside Libby, with Janie holding her hand as the constable questioned her.

'Are you able to tell me what happened?'

In slow, broken phrases Libby attempted to describe what she had seen as a result of following Bryony.

'And you say your friend lost control of her car?'

'She told me she had her foot hard down on the brake but the car just kept going faster and faster.'

WPC Williams flicked her notebook closed. 'It might be best to get these cuts and scratches seen to, Miss Frobisher. Perhaps someone could drive you to the hospital?' The policewoman looked across at Janie.

'I'll take her. Is it okay for us to leave?' Janie said.

'I can't drive, Janie. Please don't make me drive.' Libby grabbed Janie's arm.

'Ssh now, I'll drive your car. It's not a problem.'

'I'll take a brief statement from you, Mrs Juke, confirming what you told us during your phone call,' the constable said, 'then it's fine for you to leave.'

Janie ran through the events of the last few hours, while the constable made notes.

'You all arrived at the same time yesterday afternoon? And it was before supper when Mr Bramber told you he was going out? So that would be...?'

Before Janie could answer Libby said, 'It was just before six.'

'It was you he spoke to? Can you tell me his exact words?' The constable addressed Libby, who responded by closing her eyes.

'Constable Williams,' Janie said. 'My friend is still in shock. She's struggling to think straight. But I'm sure that John said nothing about where he was going. Just that he was fetching something from his car and he'd be back for supper. That's right, isn't it, Libby?'

Libby nodded, opened her eyes, and looked down at her blood-stained jacket.

'Janie.'

It was as if Libby had been transported to an alternative universe where nothing made sense.

Janie gripped Libby's hand more tightly. 'Don't worry about the jacket, don't worry about anything. We'll make it right, you'll see.'

Turning to the detective Janie took the wallet from the deep pocket in the front of her duffel coat, handing it to the constable who slipped it into an evidence bag and zipped the bag closed.

'John's wallet. We've all touched it, I'm afraid, Detective Inspector. We were with Will when he found it. We showed it to Clem and the others when we got back here.'

'Came across it by chance, did you, Mr Torrance?' Cooper said.

'Yep, but Detective Inspector, would it be alright if I phone Mrs Bramber?'

'Best to leave that to us, son. We'll be making a visit to Mrs Bramber shortly. Before we go is there anything else any of you can tell us about yesterday evening, your last sighting of Mr Bramber?'

'Olivia, you said you saw John speaking to someone outside. Do you remember?' Janie said.

Olivia's response was to make a detailed inspection of the mother-of-pearl buttons on the cuffs of her blouse.

'Another person, you say? I'll need a description. Exactly what time was it you saw them speaking together?' the detective asked.

'I just said I might have seen someone. Really, I'm so flustered. I'm not sure what I saw and what I didn't. I must say, officer, I resent you interrogating me as though I'm a criminal. In fact, the whole thing has given me quite a headache. I'd like to go to my room. I need to lie down.' Olivia brushed her forehead with the back of her hand, before strutting off; an actress leaving the stage after the first act.

'Right-ho. Now, what about the rest of the delegates? Are they likely to have any information for us?'

'I haven't told them anything about it,' Clem said. 'It's better if they are able to continue with the conference without any interference. They won't be able to help, they had nothing to do with John.'

'I think we should be the judge of that, Miss. But first I think we need to look at Mr Bramber's car, then we'll visit his home and speak to his wife. Mrs Juke, you can drive Miss Frobisher to the hospital when you're ready.'

'Sir,' WPC Williams stepped forward. 'Should we look at the other car, the one that sped out of control earlier?'

'Quite so, Constable. We'll do just that. Mr Torrance, with us please. We'll drop you back here once we've inspected the site of the two cars. From there we'll visit the Bramber house, speak to Mrs Bramber, and then on to the hospital. All being well we'll be able to speak to Miss Sandwell. We will need to take brief statements from everyone, but we can do that later once we've gathered the initial facts.'

Alison had been missing since the arrival of the police officer. Now she came through from the kitchen, attracting the attention of the detective.

'Ah, and who do we have here?'

'Mrs Alison Newman.'

'Been hiding away in the kitchen have we, eh?'

'I haven't been hiding anywhere.'

'We'll need to speak to you, Mrs Newman, but later. Let's take a quick look in Mr Bramber's room before we go.'

'I can take you to his room,' Will said. 'It's next to mine, over in Park Village.'

'Lead the way,' the detective said, turning back to face the others. 'I'll be back later today to take detailed statements from the rest of you. So don't think of going anywhere until then, eh?'

CHAPTER 12

DESPITE THE HEAVY TRAFFIC, the drive into the centre of Brighton took Janie little more than ten minutes. No doubt with Libby driving it would have taken much longer. On this occasion, though, Libby was content to sit in the passenger seat, saying very little. Several times during the journey Janie asked her friend if she was alright, with Libby's response a quiet nod.

The hospital was well signposted from the main road and as Janie pulled up in front of the impressive Regency style building, she was taken aback. The four storeys, the beautifully designed frontage, suggested to Janie she was looking at a museum or a theatre, rather than a hospital. But then her focus was on following the directions to the public car park. While Libby was in need of nursing attention, she couldn't be classed as an emergency and somehow driving into the parking bays next to the ambulances felt like an imposition. Instead, once parked, Janie helped Libby from the car. While her arms were badly cut and scratched she appeared to have no injuries to her legs, although the shock of the crash had left her very unsteady. With her acknowledged fear of driving, watching a car spinning out of control must have been one of her worst nightmares.

The assistant on the reception desk smiled as they approached.

'Can you direct us to the minor injuries unit?' Janie asked.

'Along the corridor, first left. You can't miss it.'

'Also, a Miss Bryony Sandwell was brought here by ambulance earlier after her car crashed. Are you able to tell us which ward she's on?'

The woman looked down at several sheets splayed across her desk. 'And you are?'

'Her friends.' These were the first words Libby had uttered for some time. 'I was there when she had her accident. I was with her until the ambulance arrived.'

The woman nodded and looked again at her paperwork.

'Miss Sandwell has been admitted to intensive care. You won't be able to see her, I'm afraid.'

'Intensive care? But she was talking to me. She was conscious.' The panic in Libby's voice was quick to surface.

'Try not to worry. If she was in a car crash, the chances are she could have suffered a head injury. In those circumstances the patient would be admitted to intensive care for monitoring. The doctors will discuss everything with her next of kin.'

'We don't know if she has any next of kin,' Libby said.

'I'm afraid I can't tell you anymore. But as her friends, perhaps the best thing you can do is to see who might be her nearest and dearest. There must be someone?'

Janie thanked the receptionist and pulled Libby away.

'Stupid. I'm so stupid,' Janie said. 'I should have asked Clem about Bryony's family. I'll book you in with the minor injuries unit, then I'll ring the university, see if I can get hold of Bryony's contact details.'

Leaving Libby in the care of a nurse, Janie used the public phone box in the hospital reception to call Clem.

'What do you mean they won't tell you how she is?' Clem said.

'They'll only speak to her next of kin.'

'Ridiculous. These places. All they think about is their precious rule book. All the rule books need burning, we have to start afresh, rethink everything. People should be at the heart of decision-making, not bureaucracy.'

'I can hear how passionate you feel about it all, Clem, but this isn't the time to worry about changing the world order. Do you know Bryony's family circumstances? Do you have a phone number for her, or an address?'

Silence at the other end of the phone did little to reassure Janie.

'I'll have to look through my papers. She might have provided a contact address when she confirmed she was attending. Although, to be honest I wanted that side of things to be informal.'

'But you knew Bryony from before.'

'Way back, yes. But we haven't kept in touch.'

'She's not married?'

'I'm pretty sure she's not married.'

'Does she still live with her parents?'

'I honestly don't know.' Janie detected genuine concern in Clem's voice. 'I'll see what I can find out. I'll speak to the others too. But our best hope is that we can speak to Bryony once she's well enough.'

As she hung up the phone Janie tried to shake off a sinking feeling in the pit of her stomach. So much had happened in less than twenty-four hours. One person missing, another badly injured. Could the two events be connected? Libby had said that Bryony's car was old and full of rust, so it made sense that the failure of the brakes were nothing more than a mechanical problem. Nevertheless, there was clearly tension within the group, a shared past each of them seemed loath to talk about.

She retraced her steps to the minor injuries unit where she found Libby being tended to by a nurse who had somehow managed to get Libby laughing.

'And then, you'll never know what the silly cat did?' The nurse had a strong Irish accent and reminded Janie of one her favourite library customers who was always full of beaming smiles, despite enduring a whole range of hardships.

'Malcolm sounds like one crazy cat,' Libby said, seemingly unaware of the antiseptic being applied to the cuts and grazes on her hands and up her arms. 'Oh, Janie, you must listen to this story.

Nurse Jean has the craziest cat. I mean really, calling a cat Malcolm is mad enough.'

As Nurse Jean continued to clean Libby's injuries, she recounted the rest of the story about her pet, which seemed to be the archetypal version of a cat with nine lives.

'And so, he survived the fall from the pantry window?' Libby asked.

'Landed in the wheelbarrow, which was still filled with compost. He's indestructible that one,' Nurse Jean said, as she finished applying lint to the worst of the cuts before covering them with a small bandage.

'Much like my friend, Libby,' Janie said, putting an arm round Libby's shoulder. 'Look at you, almost as good as new.'

'Thank you so much.' Libby held out her hand to shake the hand of the nurse. 'You've healed me in more ways than one. I don't mind admitting I felt a little overwhelmed when I arrived.'

'Shock does strange things to people. But a good chat and a bit of a laugh can often be just the ticket,' Nurse Jean said. 'Now your friend is here, I'll leave you. Take it easy, go home and have a rest if you can. It might take a day or two to really feel yourself again.'

By the time they were back in the hospital car park Janie had updated Libby on her conversation with Clem.

'So, we don't know any more. Not how Bryony is, or why she was driving off like that?' Libby said. 'She'd probably had enough of being ignored and was heading home. It's not as if any of her so-called classmates were holding out a hand of friendship.'

'All we can do is guess, until we can speak to her. But DI Cooper said he planned to come here to talk to Bryony. Let's grab a drink and something to eat. There's a café near the entrance. If we sit there we're bound to see him when he arrives.'

Two cups of tea and several packets of biscuits later they watched as Cooper came in through the main hospital entrance, accompanied by the uniformed constable.

'Mrs Juke. You're still here.' The detective approached the table, looking down at the empty biscuit wrappers sitting in the saucer of

Libby's tea cup. 'Good idea. Tea and biscuits, eh? Perfect to calm the nerves. I've visited the site of the incident with Miss Sandwell's car. Not a pleasant thing to witness, that's for sure.'

'Was it an accident, officer?' Janie asked.

'What makes you ask that?'

'We were thinking it's quite a coincidence,' Janie said. 'John Bramber's car comes off the road somehow and ends up in the woods, then Bryony's brakes fail.'

'Got a taste for intrigue, have you?'

'We've some experience with crime investigations. We'd be happy to help.'

'Experience, eh? And what makes you think we'd want to involve civilians in the gathering of evidence? If you've had "some experience with crime investigations" as you put it, you'll know the best thing you can do is leave us to do our job.'

'We don't mean to interfere, but if we can help with anything...' Janie's voice petered out as the detective held up his hand, stopping her mid-sentence. Nevertheless, she continued. 'Bryony is in intensive care. No one is allowed to speak to her. We thought if we could track down her family...'

'No husband then?'

His question led Janie to reflect. If she and Libby could tease out the truth about whatever went on in the past between the various members of the debating group, it might lead to something useful. Something they could present to the police that would help with their investigations.

'We'll go back to the university and see if Clem knows anything that might help,' Janie said at last.

'I'll be returning to the university later today to take detailed statements from the others. You can tell me then about any further information you might have gathered.'

It seemed that no further admonishment was coming. Instead Cooper appeared to be sanctioning their involvement, at least for the moment.

'Before we go,' Libby said, holding Janie back. 'You didn't say whether you found anything of concern when you checked Bryony's car? Anything that might have caused the accident?'

'Oh, it was no accident, Miss. Oh no. The brake pipe has been cut right through. Someone wanted Miss Bryony Sandwell to crash. Now we need to find out who.'

CHAPTER 13

ON THEIR RETURN TO Falmer House the only member of the group in evidence was Will. The chill breeze that had kicked in around lunchtime had gathered momentum over the last hour or so, funnelling through the campus, making the area outside the main university building feel more like October than April. Will still wore the woollen poncho over his cheesecloth shirt, although his feet remained bare. Perched on the front wall, he looked up as they walked towards him.

'Libby, are you okay?' He moved towards Libby, stopping short of putting an arm around her. 'Did the cuts need stitches?'

Libby walked around him, taking a seat on the wall with Janie standing beside her.

'And Bryony? Any news on how she is?'

'It's bad, Will. She's in intensive care,' Janie said.

'Dear God. That's terrible. What have the doctors said? She'll pull through, won't she?'

'They won't tell us anything. They'll only speak to her next of kin. That's why we're back here, to see if Alison or Olivia can throw any light on Bryony's home circumstances. I rang Clem from the hospital, but she seems clueless. At least, if she knows anything she's not prepared to share it with us.'

'Olivia is still in her room, nursing her headache. I'm not sure where Alison is.'

'I wish everyone would be honest with us,' Janie said.

'What do you mean?'

'They all know Bryony and you would think with all that's happened they would want to help. The poor girl is lying in a hospital bed fighting for her life, yet they seem intent on keeping up a wall of silence, offering half-truths. Surely whatever happened in the past is gone and should be forgotten.' Janie kicked at a stone lying beside the path, it ricocheted against the wall and bounced back, catching Will on the side of his foot.

'Steady on there,' Will said. 'These feet are the only ones I've got.' He bent down to rub the edge of his foot, then looked up again smiling. 'It's okay. I won't hold it against you.'

'And then there's you and John, and more importantly, John's wife,' Janie continued. 'We can only take your word for it that you haven't planned something to remove John from the equation.'

While Janie and Will were exchanging figurative blows, Libby was quiet, her bandaged arms resting in her lap, her focus down at the ground. Suddenly, as if she was unaware of the direction of the conversation going on around her, she said, 'The police say someone tried to kill Bryony.'

The statement hung in a surrounding silence, the significance of the words making each of them still for several moments.

'Is that what they've said?' Will said, at last.

Janie nodded. 'They say the brake pipe had been cut. But who would want to do such a thing? Until everyone is honest about what they know, who they know and why, we're never going to get to the truth.'

'Isn't that the job of the police?'

'If we can help the police, speed their investigation along, perhaps we can prevent another tragedy,' Janie said.

'What are you saying? That we're in the centre of an Agatha Christie murder mystery, where we're going to be killed off one at a time?

'And Then There Were None.' Janie said.

'Janie is a world expert on the Queen of Crime,' Libby said.

'And Then There Were None, was the story where eight people arrived on an island off the Devon coast, only to be killed off one by one,' Janie said.

'Great, so who's next?' Will said. 'And how come you know so much about it?'

'She's not just a librarian,' Libby said, glaring at Will. 'She's pretty good at solving crimes. We both are. So why don't you start talking and get everything out in the open? Let's work together to make sure we don't have any more calamities. I'm sure none of us wants that?'

'Let's go inside, it's too cold to sit out here,' Will said, gesturing towards the entrance to Falmer House. 'We might even manage to persuade the kitchen staff to rustle up a hot drink for us. Hey, if we're really lucky there might be some food knocking around.'

Libby and Janie followed Will into the building and through into the refectory, where they took a seat at the same table they had been eating at earlier that day. To Janie it seemed like days rather than hours ago that they were all together enjoying breakfast.

'Shall I go and see if there's anyone in the kitchen?' Janie said.

'Let me get this off my chest first, then I'll go in search of refreshments. By that time you might feel you need alcohol rather than tea,' Will said, dragging a chair to the window, keeping his back towards Janie and Libby as he spoke.

'John and I were at grammar school together. In the same year, although he was always top of the class and I tended to gravitate to somewhere near the bottom. We were both good at sport though, usually in the same team for football, and always vying for first place on sports day events.'

From where Janie was sitting she could tell Will's focus was into the distance, beyond the surroundings of Falmer House.

'Helena went to the secondary modern, just up the road,' Will explained.

'With Clem and the rest of them?'

He nodded and continued. 'Some of us grammar school boys used to hang around the school entrance around the time the girls were headed home. Helena was a stunner. Loads of boys fancied her, but she used to be quite shy back then. She'd come out of school, arm in arm with one girlfriend or another and walk straight past us. Head down, never responding to anything anyone said to her.'

'Sounds a bit like me at that age,' Janie said. 'Some days I'd go out the back entrance of the school to avoid the boys. Mostly I just never knew what to say to them.'

'Helena was the gentlest of creatures. She had this way of looking up through her long eyelashes, and if you managed to catch her eye you'd feel as though you'd won the football pools.'

'You were smitten,' Libby said. 'And John the same?'

'No, John was cool. Made out he wasn't interested, that he was only hanging around to give me moral support. Then, we had our school sports day, family and friends all invited. Plus the kids from the secondary modern. It was a regular thing, each year they'd come to watch us compete, and we'd do the same on their sports day. There was always plenty of jeering, as you can imagine. John and I were entered in the hundred metre sprint. It was his best event, I was better at the longer distances. Anyway, when we were on the start line, we saw Helena there at the front of the crowd. Maybe it was her being there that gave me the incentive, but I ran the sprint of my life that day and beat John by quite a margin.'

'He wouldn't have been happy with that,' Janie said.

'Even less happy when Helena ran over to me and threw her arms around me, laughing and telling me well done. Winning that race was great, but having her right there congratulating me... that was the best prize.'

'And John?' Libby asked.

'He laughed it off. Said he wasn't on the best form, that next time he'd beat me no problem.'

'You dated Helena after that?'

Will remained at the window, still with his back to Libby and Janie. When he next spoke his voice was muffled, as though he was merely speaking his thoughts out loud.

'One year. One blissful year. We were inseparable, couldn't get enough of each other. Even doing our homework together. She was brighter than me, such a whizz at maths and science. Me, I couldn't tell you what a quadratic equation is for love nor money. But Helena loved playing around with numbers, said it was like the best of puzzles.'

'And then?' Janie said, almost loath to interrupt Will's story.

'I never discovered the truth of it. I called round her house one day and she announced she didn't think we should see each other again. Just like that.'

'She gave you no reason at all?' Libby asked.

'She said her parents wanted her to concentrate on her studies, that having a boyfriend was too much of a distraction.'

'Perhaps that was the genuine reason?' Janie said.

Will shook his head, turning to face them, his eyes clouded.

'Two weeks later I saw her in town with John. And that was pretty much it. A year later they were engaged, a few months after that he handed me an invitation to the wedding.'

'I don't know which of them is worse,' Janie said. 'Helena for lying to you, or John for stealing her from you.'

'I'm guessing your friendship with John ended once you discovered he'd stolen her from you?' Libby asked.

'I only ever had one conversation with him about it, soon after I saw them in town together that first time. John just laughed, said something along the lines of all being fair in love and war. After that I avoided places where I thought I'd bump into them. We'd all left school that summer, but Helena and John went on to college and I managed to get a job out of town with digs thrown in.'

'And the wedding?' Janie asked again.

'I took the Magic Bus down to Greece. Left the day before the wedding. Spent the last five glorious years bumming around the Greek islands, bar work, any work I could get. I slept on friends' floors, or on the beach some nights.'

'And the commune? You mentioned something about that yesterday?' Libby asked.

'Yeah, it was like a commune. Just a load of like-minded people wanting a simple life.'

'What made you come back? And why come here this weekend?' Janie asked. 'Was it finally to get revenge on John, for stealing Helena from you?'

Will gave a little laugh. 'No, Helena was my first love right enough. But my time in Greece taught me that life's too short to hold on to grudges forever. I thought it was time to put all that behind me, clear the way for the future. When I got back in touch with John, he said he was coming here for the weekend. It seemed like the perfect place to get to know each other again. Somewhere neutral, just him and me, no Helena to complicate the issue.'

'And within hours of your arrival John disappears,' Janie said.

'Yep. And Helena will be distraught. So whatever that detective says I'm going to see her.'

'Won't that be difficult? Isn't there a danger of opening old wounds?' Libby asked.

'Difficult or not, that's what I plan to do. But you can take me out of the frame for whatever might have happened to John. Whatever I think of him, I could never hurt Helena like that. I just couldn't do it.'

CHAPTER 14

BACK IN THEIR ROOM after Will's outpouring Janie and Libby had differing opinions about all they had heard.

'I'm inclined to believe him,' Janie said.

They were sitting side-by-side on Libby's bed, propping themselves up against the wall, with their legs stretched out. Janie had left space between her and her friend, conscious that Libby was still nursing injuries, injuries that now and then made her pull a face as though in pain.

'That's because you always see the best in people,' Libby said.

'Not always, I had my doubts about Owen Mowbray remember? And Luigi Denaro.'

'True. But the way I see it, Will has everything to gain by getting rid of John and then coming to Helena's rescue, offering her the perfect shoulder to cry on.'

'That's because you like John. In my opinion someone who could do that to his best friend is not a very nice person.'

'So he deserves to die?'

'Er, no, I wouldn't go that far. Remember, we don't know that John is dead. Let's really hope he isn't for everyone's sake.'

'You've got to admit it would be very convenient for Will, wouldn't it?'

'He seems such a genuine person, I can't believe he'd be able to tell a story like that and not let something slip. Something that would show he was lying.'

'He couldn't hold eye contact with us for most of the time. That's a clue, isn't it? I mean you know all about body language and how it can give criminals away.'

'Libby, you're forgetting something,' Janie said, tapping her friend on the leg.

'And what's that, Mrs Hercule Poirot?'

'Bryony. Someone tried to kill her. There is nothing to connect Will with Bryony and certainly nothing to suggest he might want to kill her. And I'm convinced the two events are connected – John's disappearance and Bryony's crash.'

'One person guilty of both?'

'I'm sure of it.'

'Okay, so what might connect John and Bryony? We need to guess at a motive, a reason why they've both been targeted.'

A tap on the door startled them both.

'Can I come in?' It was Clem's voice.

Without waiting for a response Clem pushed open the door. 'You two look pretty comfortable there,' she said.

'What is it, Clem?' Janie said.

'I've been through the paperwork again, but I can't find anything that might lead us to any contacts for Bryony, not even her home address.'

'So we're no further forward.'

'But the police are back. That's what I've come to tell you. They're speaking to Alison at the moment, then they'll want to speak to you both.'

'And you?'

'Yes, me too, of course. But first I wanted to clear the air with you...' Clem sat on the other bed, mirroring Janie's position. 'Looks like the hospital did a good job with your injuries?' she said, nodding towards Libby, who made a point of looking away.

'You said you wanted to clear the air?' Janie said.

'I haven't been very friendly and for that I apologise.' Her tone was stilted, as if she was reading a speech someone else had written for her. 'This conference has been a huge undertaking, so much organising. And the cause is very dear to my heart so my focus has been on ensuring the weekend goes off smoothly. I've tried to separate that from any personal relationships I might have with members of the group. I know I might have come across as harsh, but anyone who has achieved significant social change has done so by putting popularity to one side. The cause is more important than our individual sensitivities.'

'Okay, point taken. But let me ask you one thing, is this a first for you, organising an event like this?' Janie asked. She had some sympathy with Clem on that front; she was still developing her skills when it came to questioning people who might be guilty of a crime. Janie had no formal training in any aspect of detection work, having garnered all she knew from reading and re-reading Agatha Christie novels; marvelling over the skill of Poirot to tease out the truth that led him to solving the crime. She still had a lot to learn, she knew that. Perhaps Clem had taken on more than she was prepared for when she announced a follow-up to the Oxford Women's Liberation Movement weekend. While her passion for women's rights, for equality, had been the driving force, she'd clearly given little thought to the practicalities of managing a group. There were certain techniques for being an accomplished facilitator, encouraging everyone to get involved, not letting your own opinions overshadow others.

Clem got up from the bed and Janie thought she might not get a reply to her question, but then Clem said, 'I was overly harsh when I accused you, Libby. I have come across reporters who have their own negative agenda, but I know there are others who have fought hard to expose injustice. And as far as John is concerned, let's just say I know everyone well enough to be certain that no one here would wish any harm to come to him, or to Bryony. As far as John's crash is concerned, either some stranger chose to run him off the road, or he'd had one too many and he lost control of the car and ran into that tree on his own. I think the latter is more likely. And after that, I'm sure someone must have picked him up. He'll be nursing his sore head somewhere, you can be certain of it.'

'And Bryony?' Libby said.

'I'm amazed that car of hers was still running at all, it's so old, virtually falling apart, that'll be the reason for the brakes failing.'

'That's where you're wrong, Clem,' Janie said. 'The police have confirmed it was no accident. Someone had tampered with the brakes. Someone wanted Bryony to crash.'

Saying it aloud brought a reality to the situation that gave Janie a chill. She waited for Clem's response.

'That girl's life has been one drama after another,' Clem said at last.

'What is the matter with you?' Libby was on her feet, fronting up to Clem, who stood feet away from her. 'Have you no empathy? Bryony is unconscious, she might not even pull through and you talk as if it's all her own fault.'

Janie moved to stand between them. The space between the two beds in what was already a small room, meant all three were standing so close together they were almost touching.

'The police will want to speak to us,' Clem said, edging towards the door. 'Best not keep them waiting.'

'That went well,' Janie said, once the door was closed behind Clem. 'Her causes certainly take priority and she's clearly not bothered about coming across hard-nosed. But did you notice the books on the desk in her bedroom when we were in there earlier?'

'There speaks a librarian. You notice books, despite everything crashing down around us.'

'She had several books by Bertrand Russell.'

'Hasn't he just died? I remember reading his obituary, but to be honest I didn't take it all in.'

'He was famous for his pacifist views, he attended an anti-nuclear demo when he was nearly ninety and almost got sent to prison for it. Some say it was his intervention in the Suez crisis that saved us all from being blown up.'

'And they wanted to put a ninety-year-old in prison? God, this country is crazy. What happened to freedom of speech?'

'The thing is, if Clem is reading Bertrand Russell, the chances are it's not only women's lib she's passionate about. There was a CND poster on the wall above her bed.'

'And all this is important because...?'

'Perhaps her real intention for this weekend was to garner support for something bigger, nothing to do with equality for women. Something that would make authorities sit up and take note about the perils of nuclear warfare. And what if John disapproved and threatened to tell the police?' Janie's thoughts were developing as she spoke them aloud.

'I thought you said Clem believed in peace? Surely a violent protest would be the last thing she'd be planning? And violence against an individual...?'

'You've seen how fired up she gets when she talks. It could be that the attack on John was a spur-of-the-moment thing. And remember she mentioned having some kind of run in with the police in the past, which she later denied.'

'How would she have done it, though? John was driving his car and crashed. How could Clem have organised that? And what's she done with him? Unless she had an accomplice. You're not thinking Alison had a hand in any of it, are you?

'No, oh, I don't know. Libby, what if John's brakes had been damaged, the same as Bryony's?'

'The police would have considered that, wouldn't they?'

'Okay, let's go down and ask DI Cooper about John's car.'

'He's not likely to tell us, is he?'

'We might be able to wheedle it out of him,' Janie said, going to link her arm through Libby's before remembering her injuries. 'Sorry. Let's see if we can get you some more painkillers while we're down there. Let's hope our leader had the foresight to ensure a first aid kit is somewhere on the premises.'

CHAPTER 15

ACROSS IN FALMER HOUSE the police had returned and were questioning Alison when Janie and Libby arrived.

'Ah, Mrs Juke and Miss Frobisher. Can someone fetch Mr Torrance for me? I'm assuming he's in his room?' He looked from Janie to Libby and then to Alison.

'Will wasn't here when I arrived,' Alison said. 'I'd been in my room. Olivia said she needed to lie down, so I thought I'd make sure she was alright. She's very upset by the whole thing.'

'Ah, yes. Mrs Blythe. A somewhat delicate nature, perhaps?' the detective said, his tone suggesting more than a hint of scepticism. 'Two of my colleagues will be over later to take brief statements from the rest of the delegates and staff. And rather than disturbing Mr Torrance and Mrs Blythe, tell them we'll return tomorrow.'

Janie was surprised at the detective's relaxed attitude. Nevertheless, she was grateful for what felt like a temporary reprieve for Will, although mystified as to why she felt that way.

As the officers ushered Clem into a quiet corner of the refectory, Janie touched Alison gently on the shoulder. 'Could we have a chat?'

Alison appeared either uncertain or unwilling, nevertheless she followed Janie and Libby outside, sitting on the wall while Janie and Libby stood in front of her. Then, aware their position might appear confrontational Janie sat alongside Alison, gesturing to Libby to do the same.

'You must wonder what you've landed yourself in,' Alison said, aiming her words at Libby. 'I'm surprised you haven't headed straight home. I would if I was in your shoes.'

'It's important we stay here while the police carry out their enquiries,' Janie said, aware that at no point had she considered leaving the university, even though Michelle was constantly in her thoughts. An awareness that made her question her priorities. Shouldn't my daughter be my first and only concern? Then Alison was speaking again and Janie shook the thought away.

'I'll ring the hospital in a while. See if we can get an update on Bryony.'

'They're not likely to tell us anything, are they?' Libby said. 'I don't agree with Clem on many things, but I'm with her on the crazy rules that limit information to next of kin. If someone doesn't have a next of kin, then what?'

Alison stood, smoothing out her skirt, as if in doing so she was smoothing out her thoughts, deciding what to say and how to say it.

'Clem isn't a bad person. Quite the opposite, she has strong beliefs, and that means sometimes she comes across as harsh.'

'Will told us he and John were at the grammar and you were all at the secondary modern. Helena, John's wife, as well?' Janie asked.

Alison looked from Janie to Libby and then turned away from them both. After a few moments she said, 'Yes, Bryony too. Although she's a year younger than us.'

Alison stopped pacing and stood facing them both, as if she had made a decision. 'Look, you say you've both got an interest in criminal investigations, but I think you're seeing connections that don't exist, adding two and two and making five or six.'

'What should we be looking at then?' Libby asked.

'John is a successful business man. In the short time since he left college he's made himself a fortune. That's where you'll find your motive. Money is at the heart of this, I'm certain of it.'

'We know John's father has several businesses. Will told us that,' Janie said. 'Isn't it likely John made his money by following his father's example? Surely it's possible to make money honestly.

Success doesn't always go hand-in-hand with criminal activity, does it?'

'All I'm saying is it's worth exploring. Olivia said she saw someone arguing with John, just before he drove off yesterday. It's possible that someone tracked him down, challenged him over some promised business deal that had gone wrong. Remember that Helena rang this morning saying she had a message for John about his work. Perhaps John is involved in a deal that's gone sour.'

'I'll admit that ever since we found John's wallet I've been thinking about the possibility of a kidnap. Especially because his keys were left in the ignition, as if his kidnapper had to make a speedy getaway. Perhaps he was disturbed? And a kidnap would tie in with John's background. He's clearly wealthy. But Bryony's accident? How does she fit into all of this business skulduggery?'

Alison shrugged. 'You're assuming the same person is responsible for both incidents. Perhaps the two crashes happening within hours of each are nothing more than an unhappy coincidence. If I can squeeze any information from the hospital about how Bryony is, I'll let you know. Where will you be?'

'We're going to speak to the police briefly while they're here. After that we'll be in our room,' Janie said.

Alison nodded and walked away, leaving most of their questions unanswered.

When they walked back into Falmer House, Detective Inspector Cooper and his constable were deep in conversation. They were standing in the entrance area of the building next to a vending machine that Janie had noticed earlier in the day. Instructions set out in bold print on the front of the machine explained the process. By putting some coins into the appropriate slot you would be rewarded with a freshly brewed cup of tea. How it worked, Janie could only guess. Surely the promise of anything that would taste remotely fresh was optimistic at best.

She watched as the detective inspector dug his hand in his trouser pocket and pulled out a handful of coins. He fed several into the appointed slot and pressed a button. Both police officers, as well as Janie and Libby, looked on, as if a circus trick was about to be performed. A whirring noise offered an element of encouragement that soon something would appear from the opening at the bottom of the machine. First a plastic cup dropped down onto the small tray. Even from a short distance away Janie could see the dirty brown splashes on the front of the machine, suggesting the resulting drink would be less than enticing. When there was no sign of any liquid running into the cup, the detective inspector tutted and went to turn away, exasperation evident on his face. It was his police constable who took the initiative, giving a hefty thump on the side of the machine. A second later the cup was being filled, to the surprise of all the bystanders, and to the amusement of the police constable who allowed the merest of smiles to cross her lips.

It was only as DI Cooper took his first sip of tea that he looked across in the direction of Janie and Libby.

'There you are,' he said. 'Good.'

He gestured them towards a seating area. As Janie sat, she wondered if the design of the orange plastic chairs was an attempt to ensure students didn't waste precious time hanging around when they should be focused on their studies. A few moments sitting on such an uncomfortable seat would surely be a few moments too many. As if to confirm her thoughts she stood again, while Libby sat, as did both police officers.

'I have a few more questions for you.' Cooper said. 'My constable here will take notes.' He nodded at the policewoman who already had her notebook and pencil resting on her lap in anticipation.

'You arrived here yesterday afternoon,' he said.

'Yes,' Janie said.

'And what brought you both here for the weekend?'

'The debate. We thought it would be of interest.'

'You're into that kind of thing, are you?' He looked at both of them, his fixed expression giving no indication as to his thoughts.

'Why else would be here, officer?' Libby said. 'I mean if we weren't interested we'd have stayed at home, wouldn't we?'

The detective shook his head. 'Oh no, Miss Frobisher. There are many reasons why you might be here. A secret liaison, for example?'

'Trust me,' Janie said. 'We had no ulterior motive for attending. I'm married and Libby is going steady.'

'Ha, in my experience that means little when it comes to affairs of the heart.' He glanced sideways at the constable who kept her head down.

'Detective Inspector, you said you've established that Bryony's crash was no accident. Could someone have done the same thing to John's car, causing him to run into the tree?'

Cooper smiled. 'I like your thinking. It would certainly keep things neat and tidy, wouldn't it? Two crimes, one criminal. Same modus operandi. Trouble is on this occasion we're not going to get off so lightly. There was nothing to suggest Mr Bramber's car had been tampered with in any way.' He rubbed his hands together and looked from Libby to Janie as though he was waiting for the next suggestion.

Janie wasn't going to disappoint him. 'Have you spoken to Peter? He's the kitchen hand who took the phone call from Mrs Bramber. He mentioned she wanted to talk to her husband about his work. We thought it could be relevant. But you'll know best.'

'Thank you, Mrs Juke. Very helpful, I'm sure. Tell me, where does your interest in criminal investigation come from?'

'It hasn't been a conscious thing, I've kind of fallen into it. I suppose I'd lay the blame at Agatha Christie's door.' Janie coloured up, sensing her explanation made her attempts at involvement in real crime seem fanciful. 'I'm a librarian, you see.' She added, as if that in itself was reason enough.

'Books, eh? I have some affinity with you on that score. Nevertheless, I need to remind you that outside interference from amateurs will almost certainly be unhelpful.'

Janie could sense Libby fidgeting beside her. Now was not the time to get on the wrong side of the detective, so she nudged Libby hoping she would get the message.

'And so, if we could return to my original line of questioning,' Detective Inspector Cooper continued. 'You arrived yesterday, not having met any of the group beforehand? You had a discussion with Mr Bramber, that's correct?' He directed the second question at Libby.

'We started off in the main lecture hall with all the other delegates. Then we were told to separate into smaller groups and we joined Clem's group,' Libby said.

'What made you join that particular group? Whose idea was it?'

Libby and Janie exchanged a brief sideways glance. Perhaps now was not the time to explain Libby's desire to follow John into Clem's group. Any justification could sound like an excuse.

'It just sort of happened,' Janie said.

'Ah, I see. And the particular interaction you, Miss Frobisher, had with Mr Bramber?'

'There was no interaction. It was nothing. All he said was something like, "keep a seat for me, I'll be back soon," or some such thing. There was nothing in it that might indicate where he intended to go to, or why, and certainly nothing to explain why he didn't return.'

'And your presence at the unhappy incident today? The one that led to Miss Bryony Sandwell being in intensive care? Just a coincidence that it was you who witnessed it?'

'I'm not sure what you're inferring, but trust me, I'm nothing more than an innocent bystander. I barely know John and the only reason I followed Bryony was that she stormed out, clearly unhappy about something. I was worried about her and thought it best to follow her, just in case.' Libby faltered, aware that her reasoning sounded doubtful.

'Just in case?' the detective repeated.

'Bryony is shy. She hardly said anything yesterday at the afternoon debating session, and not much more over supper. This weekend doesn't seem like her thing at all,' Janie intervened. 'But there's history. The others knew Bryony from schooldays.' She stopped short of suggesting the detective explore the connections between the group, knowing it would likely lead to a reprimand of sorts.

The detective nodded at the constable, who in turn closed her notebook and stood.

'That will be all for now. We will continue making our enquiries. We may need to speak to you again.' And with that both police officers left the building.

CHAPTER 16

WHILE JANIE AND LIBBY were being questioned by the police, Will was cycling north from the university, up past Barcombe Woods and on towards Sayers Lane. It was a route he had cycled countless times. All his life, right up until the day he left on the Magic Bus for the Greek islands, had been lived out around these streets, these woodland hideaways. He was so sure of many of the woody tracks he could follow them with his eyes closed.

Each school day, through primary and on into grammar, he'd walk from the south end of Sayers Lane to John's house. From there they would saunter the half mile or so to the school grounds. In the early days of primary school either John's mum, or Will's mum walked with them. Once they reached their eighth birthday, they were deemed to be responsible enough to do the journey on their own. Often they would meet up with other school friends and enjoy a kickabout, leading to a last-minute dash to the school gates to avoid being late.

The days of primary school were good days. Easy days when the world made sense, everything in its place.

The weight of memories seemed to filter down through Will, a heaviness in his legs making it harder to push the pedals, even when he was cycling along the flat.

Passing the sweetshop where all the local children spent their pocket money each Saturday, Will recalled the day he and John were told they had both passed the eleven plus. It was the same day Will's dad lost his job. As a union man Mr Torrance senior had led one of the many strikes that took place the year before. Perhaps his argumentative attitude to authority contributed to him losing his position as a railway signalman. Whatever the reason, life for Will from that day on changed for the worse. His dad got occasional work on building sites, all short-lived. Most days Paul Torrance would turn up the worse for wear from nights spent nursing pint after pint in the local pub. Will watched his mum's gradual demise. Something that was so much harder to bear than the occasional beatings he would get from his dad when Paul returned from a night's drinking, barely able to stand.

Will's mum, Laura, took work where she could, trying desperately to keep food on the table and coal in the hearth. Will didn't have to worry about what his mates would think of the lines of other people's washing hanging in every room of the house because he never invited friends back to his house. Not even John.

The difference in family life for those who lived at either end of Sayers Lane was stark. The northerly part of the lane boasted imposing detached properties, set within spacious grounds. Such was the wealth of the Bramber family they had their own gardener. By contrast, Will's family home was in the middle of a terraced row, no garden, just a back yard.

Since Will had returned from Greece he'd been crashing on a friend's settee. Larry reminded him every morning that it was strictly a short-term arrangement until Will found work and a place of his own. Larry was hoping his girlfriend could be persuaded to stay over now and then; little of chance of her doing so with Will kipping on the sofa.

Will came to a halt outside No 12, his family home. At least it had been the family home until money worries and his dad's increasing fits of temper made life unbearable. When it seemed things couldn't get any worse, his mother was diagnosed with cancer. Will was fifteen when she passed away. After that it was him and his dad, living in the same house, but sharing nothing. Eating apart, circling around each other until the day his dad collapsed in the kitchen, alcohol finally taking its toll.

His dad's death another signal to Will it was time to leave, there was nothing left for him, no reason to stay.

Standing at the front gate of No 12 he scanned the house. Freshly painted window frames, a bright red door, with its shiny letterbox, indications that a house that had been brought to its knees by the desperate poverty Will's parents had to endure was thriving from the love and attention of a new family.

'Good luck to you,' Will said, remounting his bike and cycling off.

There was no need to linger in front of John's old family home; John's parents had moved on years ago, to even bigger and better things. Where they were now was of no interest to Will. They had done little to help or support him through those difficult years when Will's family were falling apart, while John's continued to thrive.

Mutual friends had kept Will in touch and told him about John and Helena's move to one of the houses on a nearby new estate. As he cycled past the advertising hoarding at the entrance to the estate that boasted architect-designed detached properties, Will's silent comment was, I wouldn't give you a penny for one. He took a left turn, then a right, feeling as though he was driving through a maze, a tangle of streets where it would be easy to lose your sense of direction.

A letterbox, set on a tall stand signalled the Bramber house. The name emblazoned in gold on an emerald green, cast iron structure that stood beside a large brick pillar. He leaned his bike up against the pillar and took in the front view of the property. Ionic style columns each side of the door frame suggesting the interior would be just as impressive. A long paved path edged with neatly trimmed box hedging led to the front door. To one side of the path a neatly laid lawn with a flower border set under the front bay window. To the other, a wide drive leading to a large double garage.

A stainless steel bell push was set on a polished block of oak affixed to the red brick. The stainless steel knocker on the front door itself seemed superfluous. Choosing the bell push over the knocker, Will announced his arrival.

As he waited for a response, he felt like a teenager again, the heart fluttering that often left him stumbling over his words in those early days of dating Helena. And then the door opened, slowly at first, with only Helena's hand visible before she pulled the door wide open.

'Will.' The quietest of exclamations, leaving him momentarily wishing he had never come. The healing of those five years in Greece would surely be undone now he was here with her again.

'What are you doing here?' she said.

Neither had moved, Helena still hanging onto the open door as though it was a prop, something to steady her at this uncertain moment. Will, stood stationary on the very end of the front path. To go further, he would need to be invited inside. It was that, or turn around, get back on his bike and cycle away, to any place where he could regain his equilibrium.

'I wanted to make sure you were alright,' he said, the words sounding feeble, unnecessary. Who was he to concern himself with her? They had been apart for years, far longer than they were together.

'You'd better come in.' Helena stepped back, gesturing to Will to pass beside her into the wide entrance hall.

They stood awkwardly, each of them waiting for the other. From there a doorway led into an expansive open plan living area. Will had never seen a home like it. The décor was bold; bright orange feature walls, complementing sunrise yellow. Pop art posters displaying shocking blocks of colour sat either side of a light oak sideboard. The dining table large enough to seat six or more. The table was set with two places, a jug of fresh water in the centre, beside a crystal vase of spring flowers. Delicate blue hyacinths, bright yellow daffodils, mixed with posies of violets. It was as if the spring sunshine that had been elusive this morning was here inside the room. Then, as if to complement all he saw, he breathed in the heady smell of garlic and oregano transporting him back to a Greek beach, sparking recent memories of fresh fish caught, gutted, and cooked on a simple fire, drizzled with the finest olive oil, scented with lemon.

'You're expecting someone?' he said, nodding towards the table. 'I'm interrupting.'

'The police were here,' she said, sitting down on one of the dining room chairs, as if relieved to have its support. Will recalled her as a slender teenager; now, some six years on she was more sylph-like than ever. Her linen dress fell in loose folds around her ankles as she sat, the thin shoulder straps exposing bare shoulders, waif-like arms. For the first time in years Will was aware of his own clothes. The poncho felt thick and cumbersome. He realised it was the first time he had been in a house with central heating. The warmth that rose up inside him – perhaps from the heating, perhaps from the sudden proximity to Helena – was almost suffocating, making his desire to hold her overwhelming.

'I just wanted to make sure you were okay,' he repeated.

'They asked me when I'd last seen John, if he'd been in touch.'

'What did you tell them?'

'What could I tell them? All I know is he left yesterday morning for the university. He told me you would be there. Are you back from Greece for good?'

Will nodded. There was too much to explain, and in some ways no point explaining anything at all.

'It's good to see you, Will. Really good.' She seemed to relax a little, her gaze focused on a fine thread coming from the seam of her dress. 'Did you speak much to John? Do you know why he left like that, where he was going?'

'There wasn't much time, he left before supper on the first evening. And then we found his car...' He stopped mid-sentence, uncertain as to how much the police might have shared with Helena.

'Yes, the police told me about the car. They said he'd crashed it into a tree.' She stood and wandered over to the window, looking onto a back garden laid out with precision, borders with flowers and shrubs planted in subtle colour groupings. It was like looking at a painting.

'He could be lying hurt somewhere. I couldn't bear it if...'

Will moved towards her, then thinking better of it, he sat at the table, reminded again of the two places that had been set, the cooking smells coming through from the kitchen.

'You're expecting a visitor, I should go.' Although his words suggested a parting, he remained motionless. 'Try not to worry. I'm sure he's fine,' he continued after a few moments. 'You know John. He always comes up trumps one way or another. Have you rung around his friends? How about his parents?'

She turned back to face him. 'I called a friend. After the police left, I didn't want to be on my own.'

Neither of them spoke. He allowed his gaze to study her face, her hazel eyes skilfully underlined with fine eyeliner, her eyelashes long and dark with mascara, the palest of lipstick. As she started to speak he quickly looked away, as if he was a schoolboy caught misbehaving.

'You'll let me know if you hear anything?' she said at last.

'Of course, yes. And the police will be in touch again, I'm sure.'

Minutes later he was cycling away from the estate, with a sense the Helena of his memory, the Helena he had kept on a pedestal for so many years, no longer existed. With each push of the pedal, the loss he had wrangled with for so long was being replaced with something else. He couldn't put a name to it, not yet, but he was certain he was a step closer to doing so.

CHAPTER 17

INVESTIGATING A CASE INVOLVING a missing person was Detective Inspector Cooper's least favourite type of investigation. He'd worked on plenty over the twenty years since he'd become a detective. Questioning witnesses or suspects for any type of case meant sifting through their responses to determine what was truth, what were lies, and perhaps most frustratingly what was left unsaid. But it seemed to him that when it came to a missing person, people swiftly closed ranks. Often there was no crime scene, little physical evidence to explore. As such it left an air of suspicion to hover over everyone connected with the missing person. Cooper knew that when someone sensed they were being accused of a crime, they acted in a guilty manner, skewing their usual character. The most innocent person could appear the most guilty. The reverse was also true; the criminal could be the very one who appeared in control, as white as the proverbial snow.

These contradictions made tracking down a missing person particularly challenging. Add into the mix that a missing person often turned out not to be a victim at all, but someone who had chosen to disappear, to leave one life behind and start another, untainted by past misdemeanours or sadnesses. Nevertheless, Cooper had a duty to investigate.

To complicate matters this particular case involved a wealthy businessman. As soon as the phone call had come into the station earlier that day and the name of John Bramber was mentioned, Cooper sensed the investigation would present its own challenges.

Before he left for the university Cooper had made a few enquiries. The Brambers were well known locally. Mr Bramber senior owned a local greyhound track, as well as several betting shops. It seemed John Bramber was now responsible for running three of the betting shops in central Brighton. No reason to assume that in itself went hand-in-hand with corruption or skulduggery. Cooper would keep an open mind on that score. But money often led to jealousies of one kind or another. It was likely the Brambers had gained enemies. Since the 1960 Betting and Gaming Act had legalised high street betting shops punters had the opportunity to bet on their favourite dog by just strolling down the high street. Plenty of betting shops had opened over the last few years.

The Brambers were doing okay on both fronts, with Bramber senior still making money from a thriving track, while he and his son capitalised on the high street side of the business into the bargain. But Cooper had heard that some of the greyhound tracks were losing money, some had had to close completely, which was likely to leave a bitter taste on the part of those who had lost out.

Then there were the punters who couldn't walk away from the temptation of that one last gamble, throwing all their money into a bottomless pit. It was entirely possible a long-held grudge had something to do with John Bramber's disappearance. But why the young Bramber? Why not target his father, who had been the mastermind behind the betting empire for longer. A kidnapping was a definite possibility, although there had been no sign of a ransom demand as yet. There was plenty to mull over.

He had spent much of the day either at the university, or inspecting the sites of the two car crashes, and now it was time for him to take stock. Returning to the police station he nodded to two junior colleagues as he passed them in the corridor, keeping his gaze straight ahead. Inevitably, when he returned from investigating a new case colleagues wanted to update him on matters that had happened in his absence. It proved a distraction and right now he had to remain focused.

WPC Williams was already at her desk, head down, intent on writing up her notes from their earlier interviews. He was pleased she was working with him on this case. They had worked together on several cases and he had always found her professional and thorough. Brave enough to stick her neck out on occasion. Intuitive too. Cooper was convinced intuition played a vital role in criminal investigation, despite his boss, Chief Inspector Wright, having none of it. 'Trust facts and nothing but facts' was the Chief's one and only mantra. That was all well and good, but in Cooper's opinion establishing the truth was a subtle process. He liked to compare it with that of an archaeologist, carefully picking and prodding around an ancient burial site. Anyone going in with two heavy feet could destroy vital evidence. Something Williams seemed to know without Cooper having to tell her. Plus she was a good listener. Leave people space to open up and often they'll do just that.

Back in his office, he plumped down on the swivel chair and swung round to face the bookshelves. He'd brought the six-shelf high bookcase in from home on his promotion to Detective Inspector, the same day he moved into this office. His predecessor had nothing but a desk, two chairs and a rubber plant that was tended to as if it was a member of the family. Cooper moved the rubber plant out and his bookshelves in, filling the shelves with many of the books he had studied as part of his police training. Alongside those were some of his favourite crime classics; mostly Conan Doyle's Sherlock. Holmes' years as a detective in the many novels Conan Doyle penned had inspired Cooper since he was a young lad. Sherlock's cases spanned twenty-three years and as Cooper approached his twentieth year as a detective he had often reflected on the similarities of their journey. Of course, Holmes worked in nineteenth century Britain, with many of his cases set in London. A city that must have changed so significantly since then as to make it almost unrecognisable. It was an assumption on Cooper's part, because his only visit to London was as a young lad with his parents. It was the year before the start of the Second World War; London still untouched, no signs of the destruction that would soon follow. His father stood him beside one of the four great sculpted lions of Trafalgar Square, statues that sat at the foot of Nelson's Column.

'Look up there, lad' his father said, pointing to the figure of Vice-Admiral Lord Nelson.

Cooper was barely four feet tall. As he tipped his head back to peer up into the sky - a sky on that summer's day which was the brightest of blues - all he could see was the dark outline of the imposing figure.

'Duty, lad,' his father said. 'That's what Lord Nelson stood for and that's what I expect of you. Do your duty and you'll make me proud.'

Eight-year-old Timothy Cooper made a commitment to his father that he would indeed 'do his duty', with little or no understanding of what duty was or what it might entail. Eventually that commitment influenced his choice of career and when he told his father about his promotion, Mr Cooper senior patted him on the shoulder. It was the only acknowledgement his father would make that he was indeed proud of his son. His father came from a generation not used to expressing emotion, a man of very few words. Indeed not dissimilar to Sherlock Holmes who could be dispassionate and cold, becoming animated and excitable when he was engrossed in a case.

Cooper was somewhere in the middle, not unfeeling. At least he hoped his colleagues didn't consider him unfeeling. But excitable? No, he couldn't recall ever being excited, even at the conclusion of a case.

He stepped out of the office, gaining the attention of his team by a tap on the investigation board. Williams had written up a few notes on the board, a handful of names, but far more with question marks against them than concrete facts.

'Okay everyone. Let's run through what we know so far. Mr John Bramber. Twenty-three years old. Local business man, owns betting shops in Brighton. Goes to a weekend conference on women's rights, being held at Sussex University. Chats to a few people during the afternoon debate, then goes off before supper and doesn't return. His car was found later that evening, run into a tree in Barcombe Woods. Keys in the ignition. This morning his empty wallet was found nearby.

'Then, earlier today one of the group, a Miss Bryony Sandwell, takes a drive out and ends up in hospital after her brakes have been tampered with. We can't assume the two incidents are connected. It's important to keep an open mind. The conference is being attended by some sixty delegates and we will make some cursory enquiries with them at some point, but our initial focus is on the small group who were with Mr Bramber immediately before his disappearance. Williams, will you summarise what we know about the other members of the group?'

Williams stood, and spoke mostly from memory, while glancing down occasionally at her open notebook.

'Seven other people in the group with Mr Bramber. Miss Clem Richmond is the organiser. She was less than forthcoming when the DI questioned her. From one or two of her comments it seems she has been involved in protest marches in the past, CND, women's rights and so on. As a result she has a negative view of the police.'

'Negative, alright,' Cooper interrupted. 'We should look through the police records to see if she has had dealings with us before now. I had to warn her it was an offence to obstruct the police in their enquiries. When I asked her if she could think of anyone who would want to harm Mr Bramber, or Miss Sandwell, and what, if any, might be the connections between them, she responded by laughing.' Cooper stopped talking, signalling to the constable to carry on.

'Yes sir, thank you sir.' Williams looked down at her notebook. 'Her actual words were: "I'm not here to do your job for you. John Bramber was a successful businessman, probably plenty of people disapproved of him. Isn't that always the case when someone's loaded? I'll admit I find the inequalities created by our current political system a travesty. But, while I might deplore John's wealth and the injustices he might have committed to achieve that wealth, I wouldn't go so far as to wish him harm."

Williams paused before continuing to read her notes.

'Then DI Cooper asked her about Miss Sandwell, to which her response was: "Bryony? Let's just say she was at the other end of the spectrum. I was surprised to see her this weekend. I haven't seen her for years and have no idea what is going on in her life that could have led to someone wanting her dead. You'll think me harsh. But we each have to find our own way through this life. I don't expect anyone to give me a helping hand and I have no desire to be responsible for anyone else, certainly not Bryony."'

'Quite so,' Cooper said. 'So I think we've got the measure of Miss Richmond. And what do we think of her friend, Mrs Newman?'

Williams continued. 'Mrs Newman - she's a primary school teacher - appeared open and genuine in her responses. If anything she seemed more concerned about providing excuses for Miss Richmond's manner. She told us Miss Richmond had been very anxious about the organising of the weekend and, in her words, "she's not too keen on authority."'

'We didn't need to be told that, did we, Williams?' Cooper said. 'But it was interesting that when we pushed Mrs Newman on her relationship with Mr Bramber, she appeared a little uncomfortable. She told us they had known each other from schooldays and she couldn't think of any reason someone would want to harm him. All very pally, but remember we are dealing with money here. Lots of it. The only reason the Brambers are in the betting shop business is to make money and there are a whole host of reasons why they might have rubbed someone up the wrong way.'

Williams completed her summary by running through the other interviews they had completed, explaining they had yet to complete formal interviews with Will Torrance and Olivia Blyth.

While she was speaking, Cooper was reflecting on his conversation with Mrs Juke and Miss Frobisher. He'd come across people like them before. Interested bystanders, excited at the thought of being part of a criminal investigation, imagining they could contribute something useful. In his experience interventions such as these only muddied the waters, lengthening the process and hampering proceedings.

But during their earlier encounter he'd discovered Mrs Juke was a librarian. And not just a book lover, but one who had a passionate interest in the skill of Christie's Poirot. Mrs Juke had an enquiring mind and although Cooper would never admit it, he felt an affinity with her. Naturally, he'd need to warn her and her friend, the local reporter, that meddling in official police business was not only unacceptable, it could often be dangerous. But that wouldn't stop him from listening to their theories.

Mrs Juke had picked up on the possible connection between Mr Bramber's business dealings and his disappearance. She had also mentioned Peter Turnbull, the young kitchen hand who had taken the call from Mrs Bramber. Cooper had spoken with him briefly, but elicited nothing useful.

However, the business angle was a definite line of enquiry. The Brambers were rich, but wealth didn't always equal corruption. There were enough high achievers across the land who brought employment to their local communities. Nothing wrong with that.

Cooper's visit to the Bramber's home earlier that day was an eye-opener; the house and gardens oozed money. Not a cushion or ornament out of place. Light, airy, yes, but no cosy corners to relax into. Cooper could never feel comfortable living in something that more closely resembled a show home.

Cooper's own home could best be described as modest. He earned a good wage as a detective and was determined it should be the only wage coming into the household. On several occasions his wife, Miriam, had mooted the idea of getting herself a 'little job'. 'It'll give me a bit of pin money,' she argued. But each time he batted the idea away. Surely it was a man's duty to provide for his wife? The last decade had seen so much social change that he could barely keep up with it. Women clamoured for recognition, and yet, in Cooper's view women had always held the most special role in society. They were responsible for the birth of a new generation. Surely, there couldn't be anything more important than that?

Bringing his focus back into the room, he looked around his team.

'Any thoughts about what we should explore next?' He offered the question up to anyone prepared to respond.

Powell, the youngest member of his team to join the ranks of CID, held his hand up. 'Should we look more closely into Mr Bramber's business affairs? Perhaps there were money worries?'

Cooper wasn't going to dismiss Powell's suggestion, but considering the opulence of the Bramber home, if there were money worries, they were being very well hidden. Although he shouldn't discount the possibility that John Bramber had created a façade of wealth, underpinned by debt, of which perhaps even his wife was unaware.

'Worth a look, Powell. I'll leave you to do the necessary. Remember, we are also looking into the crash that nearly killed Bryony Sandwell. Are the two incidents connected? Hopefully, Miss Sandwell can offer up some pointers. We're waiting to hear from the hospital as to when she's well enough to be interviewed.'

'Several members of the group mentioned a shared history dating back to schooldays,' Williams said. 'Perhaps one of them blamed Mr Bramber and Miss Sandwell for something that happened back then? If this was the first time they'd all come together since leaving school, perhaps this person, or persons, decided it was time for them to be punished?'

'A joint venture, you're thinking?' Cooper said.

'Possibly, sir,' Williams replied.

Williams had a point, it was certainly possible the answer to today's investigation was buried somewhere in the past.

'Make your phone calls, root around in whatever records you can lay your hands on,' Cooper said. 'We'll come back together tomorrow morning and share what we've discovered. And remember, don't take anything at face value. Establish a motive and that will take us to our perpetrator.'

CHAPTER 18

THE PHONE CALL FROM the hospital came through just after five thirty. As no one had been able to establish Bryony's next of kin, the ward sister phoned the university and asked to speak to the person who had been with Miss Sandwell when she crashed.

The brisk wind from earlier in the day had not abated, if anything it was building in strength threatening a cold evening ahead. Despite the chill, Libby was out walking the university grounds with Janie when they heard Clem calling them from a distance. They stopped walking and let her catch them up.

'Bryony is out of intensive care,' Clem said. 'They've moved her onto the ward. They've contacted the police too, but the ward sister said Bryony could do with a friendly face. She's out of immediate danger, still very poorly, but they'll permit a short visit.' The information was given with a matter-of-fact tone, as if Clem was doing no more than reading out a news bulletin.

'We'll both go,' Janie said, pre-empting Libby's fears about having to drive.

'They might not let you both in,' Clem said, immediately turning and walking back into Falmer House.

'I'll wait outside the ward if I have to,' Janie said. 'Hopefully, we'll get there before the police. Once DI Cooper has spoken to her, she might be too shaken up to say much more to us.'

As they returned to their room to fetch the car keys they passed Olivia on the stairs.

'Feeling better?' Janie asked.

Olivia wiped a hand across her forehead in a theatrical fashion. 'When are we going to be allowed home?'

'When they've asked all their questions and got the answers that leads them to some sort of conclusion, I guess,' Janie said.

'Oh, these endless questions. We're not likely to know anything, are we? Why would we?'

'Didn't you say your husband and John were in business together?' Janie asked.

'I also said I know nothing about my husband's business affairs.' Olivia glared at them both and made to walk away.

Janie held her back. 'Olivia, have you spoken to your husband? Might it be worth ringing him, letting him know what's happened to John?'

'That's just it, though, isn't it? We don't know what's happened to John.'

'Isn't there a chance your husband could give the police names, people he and John have had business dealings with?'

'I'd like to know what gives you the right to poke your nose into other people's private lives.' Olivia shook Janie's hand away and continued walking down the stairs.

'Come on,' Libby said. 'Forget Olivia for the moment and let's get to the hospital. The last time I saw Bryony I was scared she might not survive her injuries. If we have the chance to speak to her, to see her conscious and hopefully recovering, it'll be the start of turning this nightmare into something a little more manageable.'

Twenty minutes later they were in the hospital foyer, speaking to the same receptionist they had spoken to earlier that day. It crossed Libby's mind that the woman had worked a long shift; she was almost tempted to ask her what time she would finish.

They were directed to Worthing Ward and told to speak to the ward sister, who stood at the doorway to the ward, a sentry, monitoring all who entered.

'You'll have to wait here in the corridor,' she said to Janie. 'Miss Sandwell is still very weak. We're only allowing one visitor at a time and only for a short while.' Then she turned to Libby. 'Don't go upsetting her, it's vital to keep her as quiet and calm as possible. Head injuries are always worrying.'

'You mean she could relapse?' Libby said, a rising panic in her tone.

'The doctor is happy for her to be transferred out of intensive care. She'll be constantly monitored. Try not to worry.'

The ward sister's words did nothing to alleviate Libby's anxiety. It was as if she was back there in the car beside Bryony, as it careered out of control. She could feel her heart thumping, her pulse racing. She felt Janie's hand on her back, gently easing her towards the swing door that led into the ward.

'You'll be fine, Libby,' Janie said. 'Just hold Bryony's hand and tell her she's going to be okay. She'll be pleased to see a friendly face.'

And then it was time for Libby to follow the ward sister into the ward, past four other beds to where Bryony was lying.

While still out in the corridor Libby had been acutely aware of the strong smell of disinfectant, mixed with bleach, that pervaded the whole hospital. Now, inside the ward, the smell was even more powerful, making Libby feel faint, reminding her why hospitals were her least favourite place.

Her first sight of Bryony, lying very still, supported with two large pillows behind her head and neck, reminded Libby of a painting. It was one of several on display at an exhibition she'd attended all about Florence Nightingale. She couldn't remember the name of the artist, but she recalled being struck by the vulnerability of the person lying in the bed. The painting was almost monochrome; white bed linen, white nightgown, the patient's face pallid and a thick white bandage around his head. The bed in the painting was iron-framed, offering no suggestion of comfort, and dark shutters at the window blocked out any sunlight, making the overall scene so melancholic.

As Libby approached, Bryony began to turn her head, but seemed to think better of it and returned to looking straight ahead, closing her eyes tight as if in pain.

'Bryony, it's me, Libby.' She laid a hand on the bedcovers, concerned that even a small movement might cause Bryony pain or distress. 'Don't try to move, you don't even need to speak. I'll just sit with you a while and if you want to doze off that's fine with me.' She tried to lighten the tone of her voice; anything to lift the spirits of the young woman who had clearly suffered, was still suffering.

'Thank you so much for coming.' Bryony spoke quietly and slowly, her eyes remaining closed. 'I hope you don't mind, but it's easier if I don't look at you. When I move my head it feels as though the world is turning.'

'You've had a nasty bang on your head. But the doctors are really pleased with your progress. That's why they've moved you onto the ward.'

'I can't remember very much. The car... you were there, I remember that. After that it's all a blur.'

'It's fine, really. Don't think about it now. The doctors know what they're doing, you'll be right as rain in no time, you'll see.'

'I was so frightened, Libby. I couldn't stop the car, I tried, really I did...'

'You have nothing to blame yourself for. There was a problem with the car, there was nothing you could have done.' This wasn't the time to tell Bryony that someone had intended for her to crash. Someone who wanted to silence her? But why? And who?

'Do you believe in fate?'

It wasn't a question Libby was prepared for, not something she had ever given much thought to.

'Perhaps in the end we're always punished for the bad things we do,' Bryony continued. 'I've done some terrible things. It's only right I should be punished.'

'Ssh now. I don't believe you can have done anything so bad you deserve to end up in hospital. This was just a terrible accident. It's really not your fault.'

'You don't know me, Libby. If you knew the truth about what I've done, about who I've hurt. They say bad people go to hell when they die, well what about a hell on earth? Perhaps that's the real punishment.' As she finished speaking Bryony kept her head still on the pillows, but opened her eyes, her gaze darting left and right as if fearing something or someone was lurking in the corner of the ward, ready to pounce.

'You're upset and that's understandable, but right now your focus must be on getting better. Nothing else matters. When you feel ready, we can talk again.' Libby stood, sensing she had already stayed too long. The ward sister had asked her to keep Bryony calm, but the conversation so far was doing just the opposite.

'Who can we contact for you?' Libby said, almost forgetting one of the reasons for her visit. 'Your mum or dad? A brother or sister?'

'There's no one.' An emotionless statement that tore at Libby's heart.

'I can't believe that. There must be someone who will be worrying about you.'

Before Bryony could respond she sensed the ward sister coming towards her, accompanied by Detective Inspector Cooper.

'I'm going, but I'll be back, I promise.' She gave a gentle squeeze of Bryony's hand, hoping to infuse her with whatever strength she might need to withstand the detective's questioning.

She passed by the detective, giving a brief nod, and then she was out in the corridor, so grateful Janie was there.

CHAPTER 19

FOR MOST OF THE return journey to the university Libby stayed silent. Janie could see her friend was visibly upset by her visit to Bryony's bedside and wanted to give her the space to mull over what had been said without bombarding her with questions. There had been enough of that over the last few hours.

It was only as they approached the campus itself that Janie realised neither of them had eaten since the soup they'd had at lunch time. She'd always found it difficult to think straight when she was hungry; something Greg often teased her about. Thoughts of Greg led immediately to thoughts of Michelle and she had a sudden desperate desire to hold her daughter, to hear her happy gurgle, enjoy the lavender and rose smell of her when she was freshly bathed. A feeling of loss washed over her, quickly replaced with a feeling of guilt. I'm a mother first and foremost. What am I doing here when I should be at home caring for my daughter?

'She seems to blame herself,' Libby said, interrupting Janie's thoughts.

'Bryony?'

'Much of what she said didn't really make sense. She was on about punishment. She even mentioned hell and damnation. I was out of my depth, Janie. You should have spoken to her, you're better at that kind of thing.'

It's strange to think of Bryony feeling guilty, when I'm feeling the self-same thing.

'She didn't give you a clue as to what she might have done to warrant punishment?'

Libby fell silent again.

They had reached the university car park. Janie pulled into a space and turned off the engine.

'I'm really hungry, what about you?' she said.

'All I can smell is bleach, it's as if clinging to me, not letting me free of it. So, no, the thought of food is not appealing.'

'Tell you what. How about we walk around the grounds for a while? It's windy enough to clear those smells away, and hopefully clear your head a bit too. Then we can go and plead hunger in the kitchen. I know supper isn't far off, but I could do with a sandwich right now.'

Libby seemed willing to be led. She eased herself out of the car, still favouring the injuries to her arms, and fell in step beside Janie.

'You don't think Bryony was saying she had something to do with John's disappearance, do you?' Janie said. 'I mean when she was on about guilt. Could she have had a hand in it?'

'Absolutely not.' Libby's response was firm. 'I can't see it. She's scared of her own shadow. Can you really see her planning John's demise? No, that's not it.'

'It looks as if we'll have to keep on at the others, try to jog their memories about what went on back then.'

'Why should they tell us anything? They see us as the enemy. At least Clem does. Especially me. She's convinced I'm only here to write some dreadful article that puts a negative slant on women fighting for equality. Although why she would imagine I'd want to do anything of the sort is beyond me.'

'That's not all of it, though. You know what I was saying about Clem's involvement with CND. A lot of those CND protests in London and Aldermaston, they weren't always peaceful, were they? If she's that passionate about her voice being heard she could be gathering support for something big, perhaps even a break-in to one of the nuclear facilities.'

'But that would be madness. Dangerous madness.' Libby slowed her pace, coming to a standstill.

'People will do all sorts to achieve their goal. All they have to do is convince themselves they have right on their side.'

'So, one theory is that Clem tried to rope some of the others into her plan. But if she was planning something big, it could be that it's the opposite; that she was trying to keep the whole thing under wraps and somehow John and Bryony got wind of it. It's all possible, but do we really think Clem is capable of attempted murder? I just can't see it.'

'I know, I guess I'm shooting in the dark. But all this makes me realise how much of a mess our world is in. I read the news, but I suppose until now I haven't thought about it in any great depth. I know that in recent years the CND crowd have put their energies behind protests against the Vietnam war and I can't say I blame them. Thousands of American men sent to their death, a whole generation. And there seems to be no end in sight.'

'Sounds to me as if you're ready to join up yourself? What would Greg make of that?'

'If it means we can achieve peace, then yes, I'm all for it. Clem and Alison are right, we need to stand up for injustice. Otherwise, where will it all end and what kind of world will Michelle grow up in?'

'I agree with everything you're saying, but right now we need to focus. Who should we tackle first?'

'Let's speak to Alison. She seems to be the most sensible of the lot of them. I reckon she's only remaining tight-lipped out of some sort of misguided loyalty to Clem. But first, let's go round the grounds one more time, then we'll go and beg a sandwich.'

As Libby's blood-stained jacket was unwearable she had reverted to wearing a fur-edged waistcoat over a long-sleeved blouse, even succumbing to borrowing one of Janie's scarves to tuck inside the collar to help fend off the early evening chill.

After another lap of the grounds they found themselves in the yard outside the kitchen. The yard was empty, but cooking smells wafted through the partly open door, drawing them inside.

'Hello,' Janie said, announcing their arrival, although she was greeting what appeared to be an empty kitchen with no cook in sight. Nevertheless, there was already a sense of comfort as they moved from the outside chill into the warm.

What must have been a door to a pantry was open and as it closed a short, stocky woman emerged. In her arms was a large saucepan filled with cooking apples.

'Oh, you quite startled me.'

The woman nudged the door closed, making her way to an area of work surface where she set the saucepan down, some of the apples falling from the pile and rolling onto the floor.

'Sorry, let me,' Janie said, bending to pick the apples up and handing them to the cook.

'One of the conference delegates, are you? You're not really supposed to be in here.' She nodded towards Libby. 'Looks as though you've been in the wars and from Peter has been saying you've all had a rough time of it. I'm Marjorie, by the way.'

'I met Peter this morning,' Janie said, briefly wondering how he knew about the events that had unfolded. 'Sorry, we should introduce ourselves, I'm Janie and this is my friend, Libby. We didn't want to interrupt your work, but we were wondering if there was a chance of a sandwich?' She paused, and then continued. 'As you say, it's been a rough day. Especially for Libby here.'

'You can't go wrong with a sugar sandwich. That's what my mum always told me. Good for energy, good to lift the spirits too. Something sweet in times of crisis, that's my motto, which is why I've decided to make an apple pie as a treat for you all this evening. Miss Richmond said it was to be fresh fruit for dessert, nothing fancy. But apple pie isn't fancy, is it? And it'll go down a lot better than a plain old apple or banana, isn't that so?'

As she was speaking, Marjorie took the lid off a large enamel bread bin, removing a sliced loaf and buttering four slices.

'Has Peter finished for the day?' Janie asked.

'No, no. He's just running an errand for me. He'll be back in a tick. The organiser lady asked us to delay supper, what with all that's been going on.'

With the sugar sandwiches made and presented on two plates, Janie and Libby were content to stand and eat them without any further conversation. As Janie took her last bite, she felt a chill draught around her ankles as Peter came in from the yard. He was carrying a pile of baking trays in his arms, which he set down on the cooker.

'Hello again,' Janie said. 'Marjorie has been kind enough to make us a sandwich, something to keep us going until supper.'

Marjorie turned to inspect the baking trays, tutting as she turned them over, as though expecting to find fault with them. 'There's a store cupboard over in one of the other buildings. For some reason, the baking trays ended up there. Lord alone knows why, or more to the point, who put them there.'

'I heard about the crash,' Peter said suddenly. 'Is the driver alright?'

'You mean Bryony? We've just come back from the hospital,' Janie said. 'She's doing okay, although it was touch and go for a time. But at least she's out of intensive care now, thank goodness.'

'Do they know how it happened?' Peter asked.

Instinctively Janie knew this was not the moment to share too much information with Peter. If the police wanted to include him when they confirmed the truth about what happened to Bryony, that was up to them.

'Now then lad,' Marjorie intervened. 'There's no point worrying about people you don't even know. You'll get yourself all riled up again.'

Marjorie turned to Janie. 'He's been a bit upset with all that's been going on out there. I keep telling him to concentrate on the cooking. In my book, feeding people with tasty food is the best way to keep them happy. If the country was run by cooks, we'd be in a better state, that's for sure.' Her laugh seemed to come from deep inside her, but ended with a raucous cough.

'It's just that I saw the woman go out in her car,' Peter said, ignoring Marjorie's advice. 'I was out having a ciggie break.' He offered nothing further, but Janie got the sense he had more to say.

'Did you speak to her?' Janie asked.

'The police told me she'd crashed. They asked me about that phone message I'd taken, but there wasn't anything I could tell them. I said as much to you when you asked me.' He glared at Janie. 'I wish I'd never taken the stupid message.'

Janie couldn't decide if Peter was being obtuse, or if he was genuinely uncomfortable with being thrust into the centre of a police investigation.

'Now, Peter and I need to get on, so if you two don't mind...' Marjorie gestured towards the door.

'Yes, of course,' Janie said. 'We don't want to delay the apple pie baking.' She smiled at Peter, before adding. 'We'll probably see you later, at supper?'

Peter nodded and once again Janie sensed he wanted to say something.

'We'll be around tomorrow too. The police won't want us heading home until they've got a few more answers to their enquiries. So, anytime you fancy a chat...'

Janie didn't wait for a reply, but followed Libby through the doorway and out into the yard where it had just started to rain.

CHAPTER 20

WITH SUPPERTIME BEING DELAYED, there was time to return to their room before supper, but Janie was still hoping for the chance to question Alison about Bryony.

If a past demeanour had led Bryony to believe she deserved to be punished, that would surely be preferable to the alternative; that Bryony could be in some way responsible for John's disappearance.

The rain was falling steadily, leading Janie and Libby to take shelter under the canopy that covered the Falmouth House front steps. Moments later they were inside the reception area. Some of the other delegates were milling around, standing in groups of two or three, deep in conversation. Janie wondered how much they knew about events to date and was briefly tempted to go over and speak to them. But what would be the point? It was unlikely they had even noticed John in the short time the whole group was together in the lecture hall on Thursday afternoon, let alone be able to contribute any useful information regarding his disappearance. She knew the police would question everyone regardless, but doubted it would add much to the investigation.

Instead she pointed to the seats she and Libby had used earlier. 'Do you want to hang around here until the others arrive?'

'How often should you take painkillers?' Libby said, as she plumped down onto the plastic chair.

'Have they worn off already?'

'How do they know where to go?'

'Who?'

'The painkillers. It's not as if you take a different one depending on where the pain is. It's one tablet that fixes everything. Or not. And right now I'd say it doesn't feel very fixed.'

'Bless you. The sugar sandwich didn't help then?'

'This long-sleeved blouse is making things worse, but it's hardly the weather for a sleeveless top, is it?'

They fell silent for a while, gazing out onto the darkening sky as dusk fell. After a few minutes they felt an icy blast of air as the main door opened and Alison came in. Standing in the entrance she shook the worst of the rain from her coat.

'April showers, I guess,' she said, stamping her boots on the doormat. 'Maybe we should ask the Chancellor to get some slippers for us, like they did in Milton Keynes.'

'We've just sneaked into the kitchen and managed to beg ourselves a sandwich,' Janie said.

'It's surprising how bad news can make you hungry, isn't it?' Alison said.

'Alison, we've been to the hospital. Libby spoke to Bryony and to be honest we're really worried about her.'

'She's out of intensive care?'

'Yes, she's being closely monitored, but they think she'll be okay.'

'Any kind of head injury is a worry. I guess they're concerned she might relapse?'

'It's what she said to Libby that's really worrying us.'

Alison had taken a seat beside Libby, but now she stood, turning to gaze out of the rain-spattered windows.

'She's in a bad place, saying she deserves to be punished,' Janie said. 'Do you have any idea why she should feel so guilty?'

Alison took a deep breath and sat again. It was as if she was preparing a defence, all the time knowing her actions were indefensible.

'You need to understand we didn't intend for it to turn out the way it did. We were young, we saw the world in black and white. We thought our opinions were right. We didn't think anything through, you don't at that age, do you?'

It was hard to guess what Alison was alluding to, so they let her continue.

'The three of us had been at Ringwood Secondary Modern since the age of eleven.'

'You, Clem and Olivia?' Janie asked.

Alison nodded. 'It was when we were in the last year, studying for O'Levels that Bryony joined the school. We didn't have anything to do with her at first. Why would we? Back then Clem was already outspoken about her political opinions. It was funny really because most of us were more interested in pop music. The Beatles had just come onto the scene, the Stones too. But Clem brushed all that aside, told us we needed to worry about the corruption in government. The press had been full of the Secretary of State for War having some seedy affair with a woman called Christine Keeler. "Our government is lying to us," Clem said. "And what other lies are they telling?" She was so passionate about injustice and she got some of us really fired up. She'd end up gathering a group around her in the playground.'

'And Bryony?' Janie asked.

'That's just it. Bryony started following Clem around, constantly pestering her for her thoughts about every press headline. She became fixated on Clem.'

'She was interested in Clem's opinion. That's not a bad thing, surely?' Libby asked.

'On the face of it, no. But Clem is not the most patient of people. And back then she had no time for hangers on. She didn't hold back from telling Bryony to clear off, it was like watching someone swatting away a pesky fly.'

'And you and Olivia?' Janie asked.

'I'll admit it. We were snobs. We knew little about Bryony's background, but we could tell from the state of her uniform, her greasy hair, dirty socks, and scruffy shoes, that her family were poor. We wanted nothing to do with her.'

'You shunned her because of the colour of her socks?' As Libby stood Janie got the impression she was about to walk away, so disgusted was she with Alison's admission.

'I'm not proud of it. We acted abominably.'

'I don't get it,' Janie said, fury in her voice. 'You're a teacher, for goodness' sake. You must know how damaging these things can be, bullying, picking on the vulnerable; for a shy soul like Bryony the hurt would have run deep. No wonder she's still afraid of her own shadow. And you're still shunning Bryony all these years on. You should be ashamed.'

'It wasn't only about Clem pushing her away, it was more complicated than that.'

'How complicated can it be?' Janie said. 'And Bryony turning up here, all these years on, is that because she still wants Clem's approval?'

'I don't know why she came this weekend. Really, I don't.'

'And you've had no contact with her since you all left school?' Janie asked.

Janie waited for a response, studying Alison's expression to elicit what the response might be.

'Bryony left school before we did. She didn't do the final year.'

Alison's constantly shifting gaze suggested she was feeling uncomfortable about what was to come next.

'She had to leave. She was pregnant.'

The statement sat in the air between them. It was Libby who first broke the silence.

'Bryony has a child?'

'She had a child,' Alison continued. 'She was fifteen, she would never have been allowed to keep the baby.'

'It was adopted?' Libby asked.

'We had no contact with her after she left. Our parents would have been outraged if they knew we had anything to do with someone who had an illegitimate child. It's not so long ago that pregnant young women were still being put into mental asylums as punishment. Incarcerated for life.'

'Dear God. And there's Clem, fighting for women's rights, for equality, prepared to shun someone who is the perfect example of someone who has been unfairly treated, who needs help. The hypocrisy leaves me speechless,' Libby said.

'Clem doesn't mean to be unkind. For her it's important to remain focused. She wants to go into politics full time.'

'I'm not sure what to think about that idea,' Janie said.

'And you're imagining Bryony believes she should be punished because she had a baby with no husband on the scene?' Libby said. 'Alison, do you know who the father is?'

'There's really nothing more I can tell you. None of us want Bryony to suffer the way she has. I feel sorry for her, really I do. It's as if a black cloud has followed her around for her whole life and it's not leaving her alone even now.'

CHAPTER 21

ALISON HAD BARELY FINISHED speaking, when the main door opened again, and the other members of Clem's group came in. Will first, with rain-soaked hair dripping onto his poncho; apparently unfazed by the downpour. Then Clem, her beret having done a decent job at keeping her hair fairly dry. She took the beret off, shaking the raindrops onto the floor, before putting the damp beret back on. The jumper she had worn since the first afternoon hadn't fared badly either, the thick Aran wool dispelling the water, protecting Clem as efficiently as the original fleece must have protected the sheep.

Finally, Olivia, whose sunshine yellow PVC raincoat, matching hat, and boots had kept her the driest of all. Libby guessed the outfit was Mary Quant or similar. Way out of Libby's budget, but that wouldn't deter her from adding it to her wish list.

'I wonder if tonight's offering will resemble edible food,' Olivia said, looking down at the mud splashes up one of her boots. 'Oh, this weather. Really, the sooner the police let us go home the better.'

'And you're imagining it won't be raining at home? Perhaps you're hoping there's some kind of divine being looking down on you, protecting you from anything that might spoil your cosy life.' Libby was still fired up from all that Alison had told them about Bryony.

She wished she could have nothing further to do with any of them. Alison's admission of guilt about the way they had treated Bryony seemed genuine enough, but words were easy. Yesterday afternoon, when the group first came together, Alison had the chance to hold out a hand of friendship to Bryony, but chose to do nothing. And Clem was so blinkered about championing her beloved causes she didn't realise how her treatment of Bryony was undoing the very causes she appeared to believe in. Equality. Sisterhood.

Then there was Olivia. Why had she bothered to turn up to the weekend? Perhaps to show off her extensive and expensive wardrobe? In a little over twenty-four hours Libby had seen Olivia in three different outfits, each one more stylish than the last.

When they took their usual seats in the refectory Olivia was directly opposite Libby, offering the perfect opportunity to question her. She waited until Olivia was looking directly at her and then she said, 'Have you always been interested in women's rights?'

'As much as any woman. Why?'

'You're right, I expect most women would say they want things to improve, but I'm not sure I'd be brave enough to go along on a protest march, though. What about you? Did you join Clem and Alison on their marches?'

'My husband wouldn't have liked that.'

'Really, why's that?'

Olivia tutted, brushing away an imaginary crumb from the table. 'He wouldn't want me making a show of myself.'

'Did your husband go to the same school as John? Is that how they know each other?'

'Roger didn't go to a state school, he had a private education.'

'Rich family then?'

'His family was comfortably off. The word rich is so value-laden, don't you think?'

Olivia was clearly hoping to maintain the upper hand in the verbal tussle.

'I guess your families mixed in the same social circles? Is that how you met?'

'I'm not sure what your fascination with my husband is, but I can tell you I'm lucky to be his wife. He's clever and extremely good-looking.'

'It's true,' Alison added. 'I've only met Roger once, at John and Helena's wedding. He was John's best man, wasn't he, Olivia? Cut from the same mould, that's what they say, isn't it? Honestly, to see them side-by-side in the church you'd think they were brothers.'

'And you've no idea about any of the business dealings your husband and John are responsible for? He's never once told you; you've never asked?'

'Roger's family owns commercial properties, not just here in Brighton, but all over the country. That's all I know.'

'Have you been in touch with your husband, Olivia?' Janie joined the conversation. 'Surely it's worth a phone call to see if he's heard from John?'

Olivia glared at Janie, then turned to the others as if hoping for back up. 'I don't know why you think you have the right to suggest when I ring my husband. You know nothing about me, you know nothing about my husband. You might like to know that it was Roger who suggested I come away for this weekend, he thought it would be stimulating, as well as giving me the chance to catch up with friends. His only concern is my happiness.'

'Ah, yes. Friends.' Libby said pointedly. 'I can see what a tight bunch you all are. Alison told us how supportive you were of Bryony when you were all at school together, how kind you were when she fell on hard times.'

The sarcasm did not go unnoticed and led Clem to say, 'Whatever problems Bryony has had to endure she has brought on herself.'

'From what Alison told us it seems Bryony's home life was difficult enough. She reached out to you, Clem. She clearly admired you for your forthright views. The chances are she thought you could show her how to turn her life around. Instead, it was as if she was nothing but a speck of dirt on your shoe, just there to be brushed away.'

'She made bad choices,' Clem said.

'We know about the pregnancy. Alison told us. But doesn't it take two to make a baby? Shouldn't the father shoulder at least half the blame?' Libby continued. 'And you're certain that none of you know who the father is? You must have seen who she was hanging around with.'

'I have no interest in Bryony's love life, not then and certainly not now.' Clem's denial came swiftly and firmly.

'And no concern for why someone should try to kill her? More than that, why they should choose to do it during your precious conference?'

'It's for the police to investigate, not for me, or any of us, to clutch at straws, or make random guesses. Do you and your librarian friend here honestly think you can do a better job than experienced detectives? I suggest you keep your noses out of other people's business and matters that really don't concern you.'

The door from the kitchen swung open, as Peter and Marjorie carried through two large earthenware dishes, the sizzle of the corned beef hash and the meaty aroma capturing everyone's attention and bringing an abrupt end to the conversation. Silence ensued, apart from Libby drumming her fingers on the table, which seemed to annoy Olivia almost as much as the verbal accusations she had been attacking her with a few moments earlier. One by one they went up to the serving counter, holding out a plate for a spoonful of the hash and another of spring greens. Collecting a bottle of tomato ketchup, Libby was the last to return to the table.

'You know, we each have a responsibility to do what we can to help the police,' she said. 'And if that means asking awkward questions, that's what Janie and I will continue to do. If you don't want to answer, that's your choice. But DI Cooper won't be quite so generous. He'll want answers and if he doesn't get them, he'll assume you have something to hide. Do you have something to hide, Olivia?'

This time it was Alison who intervened. 'Olivia will be more than happy to help the police, won't you, Olivia?' She offered Olivia her most generous smile, before holding out the ketchup bottle.

'Of course,' Olivia said, her unsettled expression contradicting her words.

Supper continued with barely any conversation, each person holding their own thoughts to themselves. It was only when Peter came over to their table to collect the plates that Janie spoke.

'Thanks so much, Peter. That was delicious and exactly what we all needed. Do say thank you to Marjorie, won't you? And we've been promised apple pie for dessert, haven't we?' As she passed her plate over to him, she held onto it for a moment longer than was necessary, catching his gaze. 'It's a long day for you, isn't it? Preparing breakfast and still here to clear up after supper. Do you live nearby?'

'Oh no, miss. I stay in the student digs, over in Park Village, Block A, ground floor.'

'Same block as us, although we're on the first floor, Room 8. That makes us neighbours.'

'We wish you a restful evening once you finish your shift.'

The others had been watching the interchange and as Peter withdrew, balancing plates and cutlery with the mastery of a circus juggler, Clem said, 'What was that all about?'

'Just being friendly,' Janie said, silently hoping Peter had understood the message that if and when he wanted to talk, she would be ready to listen.

CHAPTER 22

FINISHING EARLY ON A Friday was rarely an option for DI Cooper, or for that matter, for any of his team. Home life had to be put on hold when there was an ongoing case, which was more often than not.

He had tasked his team to find out more about the business dealings of the Bramber family and now it seemed DS Armstrong had information he was keen to share. Armstrong was like an excitable puppy, wanting to please his master. Enthusiasm was all well and good, but Cooper was constantly reminding him about the importance of thoroughness, not making assumptions. Investigations would only ever be successful if they were evidence-based, otherwise once the case got to court they wouldn't stand a chance of achieving a prosecution. Clever defence barristers had the knack of twisting facts, suggesting to the jury that black was white. Many a time Cooper had left the court frustrated at having to watch an obviously guilty man or woman walk free. He and his team might have spent weeks, even months gathering evidence, presenting what seemed like a watertight case, only to learn a key prosecution witness was no longer willing to testify, or had changed their statement completely. On some of those occasions Cooper seriously considered quitting the force. But what else would he do? He'd only ever wanted to be a policeman and with twenty years behind him and at least the same ahead, finding another career at this stage in his life was a non-starter.

No, the important thing was to be rigorous in his approach, and to ensure youngsters like Armstrong kept to the same exacting standards.

'Got some information for me, have you, Sergeant?'

Armstrong hovered in the doorway to Cooper's office, holding a notebook, which he kept looking down at as if it was a script he was attempting to learn.

'You asked me to delve into Mr Bramber's business dealings, sir.'

'I did, Sergeant. And that's what you've done, is it?'

'Yes, sir.'

'Don't just stand there. Let's update the team, shall we, eh?'

Cooper ushered Armstrong into the main office, where only two other officers were still at their desks. WPC Williams, busy typing up her notes from earlier, and Fulbright, a detective sergeant with plenty of years under his belt, but no desire for promotion. With only a few years until he could retire Kenny Fulbright didn't hide his overriding desire for a quiet life. He'd do the minimum required, keep his head down, and look forward to retirement, when he could potter in his much-loved allotment, and enjoy the occasional game of bowls or darts.

'Listen up, you two,' Cooper said. 'Armstrong has some information for us. Over to you, Armstrong. Come up here and tell us what you've found out.' He gestured to Armstrong to stand beside the information board, while taking a seat himself beside Williams. With her boss beside her, she sat up a little straighter. Cooper leant back on his chair, stretched out his legs and nodded to Armstrong to begin.

'Thank you, sir. The thing is the Bramber family is well known within business circles in Brighton. Mr Bramber senior has run one of the biggest greyhound tracks in the area for years, and then a few years back he began to open up several high street betting shops.'

'After the new gaming act, that's right, isn't it?'

'Yes, sir. The act legalised betting shops and Bramber was one of the first to grab the opportunity. Seems they are extremely lucrative.'

'Lucrative? I should say,' Cooper quipped. 'They'll be earning more than the lot of us put together. Mark my words, you'll never see a poor bookie, but plenty of impoverished punters, eh?'

Armstrong hesitated before continuing, uncertain whether his boss had more to add.

'Carry on, Sergeant. We want to know how this is relevant to the two cases we are investigating.'

'Yes sir, sorry sir.' Armstrong looked down at his notebook and continued. 'For the last few years John Bramber has been responsible for running three of his father's betting shops in the centre of town. I've visited each of them today and chatted informally to some of the punters, as well as the staff. The staff tell me John Bramber is a good boss, although they rarely see him. He calls in now and then, but mostly lets them get on. I tried to speak to some of the punters but most were loath to talk to me.'

'Not surprising, eh? There's a good chance anyone hanging around a betting shop on a Friday afternoon comes from the wrong side of the law, if you get my drift. I mean they're not working, are they?'

'They could be shift workers, sir?' Williams offered up.

'Fair point, I suppose. Picking up their wages and walking straight into a bookies to lose most of it?' Cooper's opinion of gamblers was clear. 'That's it, is it? Nothing more pertinent to the two incidents?' He waved a hand at Armstrong, as if to dismiss him, rising from his seat to indicate the briefing was over.

'Oh no, sir.' Armstrong had found his confident voice, which up until now had been hiding in the shadows. 'The chap running one of the shops, a Mr Joseph Cartwright, told me that a few weeks back there had been quite a kerfuffle.'

'A kerfuffle, eh?'

'Mr Bramber was making one of his visits. He arrived just as one of the customers was in the middle of a blazing row with Mr

Cartwright. This customer was a regular, always in the shop and losing much more than he ever won.'

'What did I tell you about gamblers? It's the same story every time. Forever holding out hope that one last bet will be the winning one.'

Armstrong continued. 'Mr Cartwright said this particular customer was accusing him of fiddling the results, holding back winnings he believed were due to him and pocketing them. Apparently the chap is local, and the word was his wife had recently walked out, taking his two children. There was also talk he was about to be evicted for non-payment of rent.'

'A sorry story, indeed, but sadly not unusual.'

Williams and Fulbright hadn't yet offered their opinion, continuing to listen intently.

'Mr Cartwright said the man became violent, taking up a stool and smashing it on the floor. Just at that point Mr Bramber came in. Bramber confronted the customer, and once the chap realised Bramber was the owner he unleashed all his anger towards him, saying things like, "you've ruined my life" and "I'll get you back one day".' Armstrong referred to his notebook again, reading the words as he had written them.

'And you're thinking this customer might have followed up on his threat?' Cooper said.

'It's possible, sir, yes.' Doubt crept into Armstrong's tone. Perhaps things were not as clear cut as they might have appeared when he made his notes.

'And you've got this man's name? His address?'

'He's a Mr Thomas Yardley. Known locally as Old Tommy.'

'An address?'

'No sir, I don't have an address. But he's well known, so it shouldn't be difficult to track him down.'

'Your job for the morning then. Williams and I will go back to the university to interview Mr Torrance and Mrs Blyth. Let's meet back here lunchtime tomorrow and see if our investigations have got us any further forward.'

'Yes, sir, thank you sir.' Armstrong moved towards his seat, but Cooper held out a hand to stop him. 'How believable is this Cartwright fellow? Did it cross your mind he might have made the whole thing up? It's equally possible that Cartwright has a grudge against his boss. Or it could be that Cartwright is on the fiddle and Bramber found out. Remember Sergeant, we can't make assumptions about any of it. We all know that people will lie to cover their tracks. It's up to us to determine who is lying and more importantly, why. Think motive. It could be money. It could equally be something else.'

Time for the team to return to their homes and families for what little was left of the evening. As Cooper put the key in his front door, he heard Barney's welcoming bark. As always on his return from work the spaniel was sitting beside his master's slippers.

'That you, love?' his wife called out from the kitchen. 'Hot milk? Or something stronger?'

'Nip of brandy in the milk should do the trick.'

Sliding his feet into his slippers and hanging his jacket up he went through to the sitting room, followed by Barney, who jumped up on the sofa beside him.

'Long day,' Audrey said, as she set a mug down beside her husband.

'There'll be another long one tomorrow.'

'I'll put some music on, shall I?'

It would be the job of Mozart to soothe the worries of the detective inspector, as he tussled the head of his ten-year-old spaniel, and tried not to think about missing businessmen, or car crashes, just for a few hours.

CHAPTER 23

IT WAS UNLIKELY LIBBY would be complaining of Janie's snoring when they woke on Saturday morning, as Janie was certain she had barely slept. Every half hour or so throughout the night she turned over and checked the travel alarm clock they had brought with them, willing sleep to come. She had phoned her dad again early on Friday evening to be told that Michelle was just fine now. She hadn't missed the hesitation in his voice.

'What do you mean "now"? Has she been poorly?'

'She was a little fractious earlier. Jessica thinks it's probably her teeth.'

'She's too young to be teething, Dad. Are you sure she doesn't have a cold? Did Jessica take her temperature?'

'She really is fine, darling. I'd tell you if there was anything to worry about.'

Her dad's reassurances weren't enough to settle the qualms she felt. What am I doing here? I should be at home with my daughter, not worrying about a load of strangers who I have little in common with and who don't even want my help.

Then late evening there was a knock on their bedroom door. Janie opened the door, not knowing who to expect. Peter stood there, colour rising in his cheeks as he appeared to struggle to form his opening words. She waited, intrigued by what he might be about to say. He'd been on the edge of both events. First, taking Helena Bramber's phone message, then mentioning he'd seen Bryony drive off. Was he merely an interested bystander, or were there connections between Peter and the others in the group? It seemed unlikely, but Janie had learned from recent investigations that it was wise not to discount unlikely scenarios. Nevertheless, she fervently hoped on this occasion her first impressions of the young kitchen hand were correct. She wanted to cross him off her imaginary list of suspects, confident in his innocence of any and all crimes.

Libby was there too, casually flicking through a magazine, looking up from time to time. This wasn't the moment to crowd the young man. If he was going to talk to them, it would have to be at his own pace.

'I wanted to explain. The thing is I recognised her,' Peter said at last.

'Who did you recognise?'

'The woman who crashed her car. Bryony.'

Janie composed herself, setting her face as if nothing out of the ordinary had been said, not wanting Peter to close down before she could completely understand what he was trying to say.

'I grew up in care,' Peter continued. 'Up until last year I lived in Claremont Mount children's home. There were around thirty of us living in a big old house, sleeping in dormitories, boys in one, girls in another. I was there from really young, but some of the kids came and went. Anyway, Thursday, before supper, I was outside having a ciggie and I saw Bryony come outside. I didn't think much about it then, but later, when I brought the food in for supper I saw her again, and that's when I realised.'

His explanation was muddled, as if Peter was sorting through the memories even as he recounted them.

'I recognised her.'

'You were in the same children's home?' Janie said.

'She's, what, seven years older than me? But I do remember her. I was maybe six when she moved in to Claremont. She only stayed around a year I think. They must have moved her on for some reason, but it's definitely her, I'm sure of it.'

'When you saw her outside, did you speak to her?'

'No. It was only when I saw her later in the refectory that I was certain. But what would I have said to her, anyway? It's not like we've got happy memories to share. She probably hated it as much as I did.'

'Did you get the feeling she recognised you?'

'Doubtful. It's ten years on after all.'

Janie's thoughts went back to Olivia's account that she had seen someone arguing with John near the alleyway leading to the kitchen. Could that have been Peter? But why would he have wanted any harm to come to Bryony? They had both suffered hardship, growing up outside of a loving family, unsure of their place in the world. Wouldn't that create a connection of sorts, two lost souls, railing against the injustices that had given them such a tough start in life?

And then, as if he read Janie's thoughts, Peter explained the real reason for his visit to their room. 'The thing is you said you help track down missing people. I want to know who my parents are, where they are, and why they put me into care.'

Janie's first thought was one of helplessness. She might have helped to track down a missing person in the past, but tracking down Peter's parents was a huge undertaking. Did she have the skills to take on such a task?

'What did they tell you at Claremont Mount? Were they able to share any information with you?'

'Before I left, I asked the couple in charge if they could give me my records. They must have records, mustn't they?'

All the time he was speaking he was looking around the room, not at anything specific, but with a constantly shifting gaze. It was as if his eyes were following his thoughts through a maze of hidden left and right turns.

Libby had abandoned her magazine to listen to Peter's outpouring. Now she chose to join the conversation. 'Your parents might not want to be found, Peter. Have you considered that?'

Meanwhile, Janie was imagining what it must have been like for Peter's mother. Was her child taken from her, as it seemed Bryony's had been taken from her? Or were they separated for another reason? Illness, or death? Such a stark contrast between the uncertain childhood Peter had experienced and the security she knew Michelle felt, being cared for by her parents, her grandfather, and her aunt.

'I don't know what to suggest, Peter. It might not be possible to find your parents. We'd have to contact the relevant authorities, understand what the law says about it all.'

'What do you mean?'

'It could be you have no legal right to the information, but I really don't know.'

'No legal right to know who my own parents are?'

'We should get Clem on the case,' Libby said, half in jest. 'She wouldn't take no for an answer.'

'Peter, you'll have to leave it with me. I promise you I'll think about it and then we can speak again.'

She watched Peter as he walked along the landing and down the staircase to his room on the ground floor. She didn't need to see his face to read his emotions, with his head bowed and his shoulders slumped forward, here was a young man who was bearing sadnesses he should never have to carry.

No wonder sleep evaded Janie.

Saturday morning dawned with the promise of a perfect spring day. The wind and rain that had hampered them throughout Friday had drifted away to be replaced with a warmth that made Janie want to linger as they made their way over to Falmer House. As she turned her face to the sun, she could sense her shoulders relax, her mind clearing.

But once inside the refectory she was faced with John's empty chair, making any brightness she felt fade away. Her hopes for the weekend, the anticipation it would give her time to think about her future had faded too. Now all she could hope for was John's safe return to the group, and a simple answer to whatever had caused Bryony to crash. Then Janie could return home to Michelle and Greg, putting thoughts of crimes, mysteries, even university study, well behind her.

The others were already seated, with plates of toast being passed around and what sounded like a comfortable chatter. But a closer listen revealed a topic that was anything but comfortable. It seemed a plan was being set out, with Clem explaining the parameters and the others muttering agreement.

'I said all along the police have no right to keep us here. I've spoken to my colleagues, the other sub-group leaders, and put them in the picture. We've agreed we have no option but to call a halt and reschedule. I'll let everyone know the new dates.' Clem brushed toast crumbs from her fingers and stretched across the table for the Marmite.

'What have we missed?' Janie said, pouring herself a mug of tea from the family-sized pot sitting in the centre of the table.

'Clem is explaining that it's inappropriate to continue with the conference, given all that's happened. After breakfast we're all going to make our way home.' It was for Alison to offer an explanation.

'You might have to wait for the police to tell us we can go.'

'All stuff and nonsense,' Olivia said. 'We've already told them what we know, which is precisely nothing. Clem is right, it's time for us to go home, leaving the police to do their job. You two might have an inordinate interest in John's disappearance, but that doesn't give you the right to ask us questions and certainly doesn't mean we have to tell you anything.' As she ended her speech, she took a breath and looked around, almost as though she was expecting applause.

'We're all concerned about John, and about Bryony,' Alison said. 'But it's as Olivia said, we'd only be wasting police time if we made random guesses about the reasons behind either event. Better to take ourselves home and wait to hear.'

Libby had yet to involve herself in the conversation, but now she stood, moving to stand beside Clem, a close presence adding weight to her words.

'You amaze me, the lot of you. So, that's it, is it? You're all happy to go back to your comfy lives without another thought for what might have happened to John or Bryony. I've been waiting for at least one of you to offer to visit her, to show some concern for her. She was your schoolmate, for pity's sake. You, Clem. You were someone she looked up to. And Alison, you said yourself you felt guilty at the way you all treated her. Isn't this the moment to make amends? If her life was going badly until this point, it's even worse for her now. Goodness only knows how long she'll be in hospital, or how well she will recover. Will, you say you and John had a falling out, and you came back to England to mend bridges. Surely a good way to do that would be to help the police with their enquiries.'

'But we've done that already,' Will said. 'I found his wallet, didn't I? There's a chance that might have given them a lead. And if his disappearance has anything to do with his business affairs, then I can't tell them a thing. I know nothing about what he's been up to over the last five years. I haven't even been in this country.' It was an impassioned speech.

'And then we come to Olivia,' Libby continued. 'Evading the police at every turn. One minute saying you witnessed an argument between John and some faceless person; but when pushed it appears that the argument might have been a figment of your imagination. Which was it, Olivia?'

'Yes, which was it, Mrs Blythe?' The solid voice of DI Cooper made them all turn towards the doorway, where the detective stood, alongside WPC Williams. 'I'm pleased to find you all here. Finished breakfast, have we? Perhaps Mrs Blythe could follow us out to the entrance area and we can have a quick chat undisturbed, eh?'

If the circumstances weren't so serious Janie might have laughed out loud at Olivia's expression, which resembled a startled gazelle.

The detective stood at the open doorway waiting. It seemed there would be a stand-off. Olivia kept a fixed gaze on her breakfast plate, despite the fact that until that moment she had barely touched the slice of buttered toast she had carefully prepared.

'If we could move things along, please, Mrs Blyth.' Cooper said. At which point Olivia stood and sauntered towards the detective as if in a dream.

'That was painful to watch,' Janie said, once Olivia and the police had left the refectory. 'Doesn't she realise the more she evades his questions the more he'll think she has something to hide?' Her question was thrown out to anyone who chose to respond, with Alison taking on the responsibility.

'You need to understand Olivia. Underneath that façade she's really very unsure of herself. She was the same at school and over the years it appears she has perfected her act.'

'Oh, I'm not staying here to listen to another story about the long-suffering Olivia,' Clem said, pushing her plate away and swiftly leaving the refectory.

'Has that always been your role, Alison? Calming the waters?' Libby said. 'I'd say Clem is lucky to have you as a friend.'

With an expression that altered Alison's appearance from confident teacher to shy schoolgirl, Janie waited for the explanation she sensed was to come.

'Clem has this way about her,' Alison said. 'She is impassioned, single-minded, and that's attractive to people who might not be so strong in their beliefs. At school Olivia was as taken with Clem as Bryony was. The difference was that Olivia came from a wealthy family and the rest of us didn't. She soon realised that bragging about being rich wasn't going to get her anywhere with Clem. The opposite, in fact. Clem has long renounced material possessions.'

'And the second-hand jumper is a reminder to anyone who might think differently?' Libby said.

'I told you before that we drifted apart when we left school,' Alison continued, ignoring Libby's remark. 'I only met up with Clem again when I joined in an anti-nuclear protest.'

'And Olivia?' Janie asked.

'Apparently Olivia had been writing to Clem on and off for the last few years.'

'Saying what?'

'Perhaps she was hoping to give some meaning to her life? I'm not sure. But when Clem decided to organise this weekend, she mentioned it to Olivia, never guessing she would come. We didn't think she'd be up for student digs type accommodation. Turns out we were wrong; she's as fascinated by Clem as she ever was.'

'What I'm struggling to understand is why Clem would have invited Bryony?'

'She didn't. Somehow Bryony heard about it, we don't know how.'

Until now Will had remained silent. Janie had almost forgotten he was there, but then he spoke.

'John told Bryony.'

His statement had everyone's attention.

'John told Bryony?' It seemed even Alison was surprised.

'I don't know the ins and outs of it, but yes. When we arrived on Thursday and I saw Bryony, I asked John about it. He said he'd told her about the weekend, thought it would be a lark for her to see her old chums again.'

It was a nugget of information that suggested to Janie she needed to look in a different direction, one that until this moment she hadn't considered, one she had an inkling may lead to an uncomfortable conclusion.

CHAPTER 24

WHATEVER DI COOPER HAD teased out from Olivia, on her return to the refectory she appeared relaxed and unfazed. Will was called through to answer questions, leaving just Alison, Janie, and Libby still at the breakfast table.

'All okay?' Alison asked Olivia.

'Yes, why wouldn't it be?'

'Does that mean we can go home? Did DI Cooper say we were free to go?'

'There's no reason for us to stay here. There's nothing more we can do, is there? I've had enough of it all, really I have. I can't wait to get home to a decent cup of tea and my own bed.'

'Did you drive here, Olivia?' Janie asked.

'I'll phone my husband. He dropped me off and he'll be here in no time.'

'I'm going to phone home too,' Janie said. 'We could walk over to the phone box together if you like, Olivia?'

'I'll come with you,' Alison said. 'Clem and I came together so I'll go and see what time she wants to leave.'

Nodding to Will as they passed through the reception area they made their way to Park Village.

Libby and Alison headed into the student block, while Olivia and Janie waited by the phone box.

'I won't be long, I'll see you up there,' Janie called out to Libby, then turned to Olivia. 'You use the phone first, I might be a while.'

A low brick wall ran all around the central courtyard to the student digs, providing the perfect spot for Janie to sit for a while, her face turned towards the sun. Although she was close enough to hear Olivia speaking on the phone, her thoughts were elsewhere. In a few hours she would be back home, collecting Michelle from her dad's, reassuring herself that her daughter was okay. Greg would probably be at football practice. She could surprise him on his return. Maybe she'd make his favourite Saturday tea; egg, baked beans, and chips. Later this evening they'd settle together on the sofa, with Michelle nestled between them for her late-night feed. With her eyes closed and the warmth on her face, Janie could feel herself drifting off. But then Olivia was beside her.

'Roger isn't there. I've had to leave a message on the answerphone.' The irritation was evident.

'Oh, well, he wouldn't have been expecting you to ring. And it is Saturday. What does he usually do on a Saturday morning?'

'That's not the point. What am I supposed to do now? You're all headed home and I'm stuck here on my own until I can get hold of him. Really it's too much.' She brushed the top of the wall with her hand before sitting beside Janie.

'Do you live far? Could Clem and Alison give you a lift?'

'I suppose so.'

'The weekend hasn't really turned out well for any of us, has it?'

'I expect you think I'm pathetic.' Olivia's tone was one of defeat, as if the moment had come for her to let her guard down.

'No one thinks you're pathetic.'

'Clem does, she always has.'

'Clem doesn't have all the answers, you know, Olivia. She isn't necessarily right.'

'I've always looked up to her, you know. People might say I've been lucky, having everything handed to me on a plate, never having to fight for a job, for a decent wage. But it really isn't that simple.'

'Nothing ever is.'

'You and Libby, you've got guts. Libby is making her mark in journalism, which can't be easy for a woman. And even though you're a mother, you're still forging ahead, carving out an independent life for yourself.'

'Hmm.' She could hardly comment on Olivia's life when she was so uncertain about her own, with doubts that had kept Janie awake throughout the night. Nevertheless, Olivia seemed to be in a receptive mode. 'It's never too late, you know. There are any number of careers you could pursue. You've got a brain, it seems a shame to waste it. What do you enjoy doing? What are you passionate about?'

'My husband wouldn't like me working. He likes his dinner on the table when he comes home.'

'Come on, Olivia, that's hardly a reason. There are plenty of part-time jobs. It's time to be brave. You might discover your husband admires you for it.'

'Can I tell you something I've never told anyone?' Olivia took a deep breath, as though still not prepared to speak aloud whatever it was she had considered sharing with Janie.

'Your secret's safe with me.' Janie patted Olivia's leg, a friendly gesture that startled Olivia. The protective shell she had maintained around herself was showing hairline cracks.

'I'm lonely.' A pause, then another deep breath. 'There, I've said it.'

'But you enjoy your husband's company?'

'He's always working, late nights, even weekends sometimes. And when he is at home, he's on the phone talking about work, or with his head in paperwork. We rarely have a conversation and in truth, I don't think he even likes me.'

'I'm sure that's not true.' It was an attempt at reassurance.

'That's why I came along for this weekend. I had this ridiculous idea that by meeting Alison and Clem again we could rekindle our friendship. But now I realise they've never considered me a friend, merely an irritation.'

Janie wanted to offer some crumb of comfort to Olivia, even though Alison had confirmed Olivia's fears to be true. The friendship had never existed and was unlikely to now or in the future.

'Just be honest with them. Let those defences down and show them who you really are.'

'I don't know who I really am. I've pretended for so long I've lost sight of the real me.'

'You said your husband was happy for you to come away on this weekend. He could probably see you've been unhappy and thought it would do you good to meet up with old friends.'

'My husband was sick of looking at my miserable face, that's the truth of it. Who wants someone moping around all day? Even I wouldn't choose to spend time with me if I could help it.'

Janie had run out of ideas. She looked down at her watch hoping to signal the conversation had come to an end, at least for now.

'I need to phone home, Olivia. Why not see if you can catch a lift with Clem, or try your husband again after I've finished with the phone?'

Janie watched Olivia enter the student digs, sensing she had done little to lift her spirits. But now her focus was on the phone call that would lift her own spirits as she dialled her dad's number, anxious to hear his reassuring voice.

'Dad, it's me.'

'Good to hear your voice, darling. Are you okay?'

'Is Michelle any better?'

'She's completely fine. A touch of teething rash making her hot, that's all. All sorted with some soothing gel. Your Aunt Jessica has it under control. You haven't been worrying, have you?'

'You know me.'

'I certainly do. And what about that missing man, and the poor girl in hospital? Any more news?'

She gave her dad a summary of what little was known.

'I'll tell you more this afternoon because I'm coming home.'

'So soon? I thought it didn't finish until Sunday?'

'With all that's happened, the organiser has decided to finish early. We can hardly enjoy constructive debates while everyone is worrying about John and Bryony. Dad, is Greg alright? You didn't mention him when I called last night.'

'He's just fine, love. He came round for supper, got treated to one of your aunt's special Italian meals. Lasagne. You wait until you've had a taste of it. It's quite something. He offered to sleep over in case Michelle was fractious in the night, but we packed him off home. He's got his football practice this morning, so he needed to be fresh for that. Anyway, like I said, your aunt is loving every minute she's spending with your daughter. Just can't get enough of her.'

'Okay, Dad, I'll see you soon. Give Michelle a big hug from me.'

'Janie, are the police making any headway? Do you get the sense they're any closer to working out what's happened or why?'

'If they have, they haven't shared it with me. But something I heard this morning got me thinking. A connection I hadn't made before now and one that could lead somewhere...'

'If you need to stay on, if you think you can help, don't worry about us because we really are fine.'

Janie hoped her dad heard her blow kisses as the money ran out. Perhaps it wasn't time to go home just yet.

CHAPTER 25

RETURNING TO THE POLICE station ready for the lunchtime briefing, Cooper was hoping his team's enquiries had proved more useful than his own.

He hadn't expected the questions he posed to Olivia Blythe to offer up much he didn't already know and he was right. Her monosyllabic responses left him wondering if she was stonewalling, or if she really had nothing useful to contribute. She continued to be vague about the supposed exchange between John Bramber and another person. If it had happened, she either couldn't or wouldn't share what she had seen, which was annoying because it presented the only tangible lead.

If what Armstrong had been told was correct and a disillusioned punter had confronted John Bramber in one of his betting shops, threatening him, perhaps the man had tracked Bramber down and had carried out the threat. There were too many unknowns. If Armstrong had been able to track down Old Tommy, there was a chance they could start to move the investigation forward.

Two detective constables had been out to the university to speak the other delegates, as well as the other organisers, with nothing useful coming from their enquiries.

Cooper had also spoken again to Will Torrance. Not much joy there either. Although he did provide useful detail regarding the relationships between most of the group, with the exception of

Libby Frobisher and Janie Juke. So often in past cases Cooper had learned that the guilty party was someone in the victim's immediate circle. Family or friend. But this time motive was thin on the ground. Will Torrance seemed to be the only one who might want Bramber out of the way. He made no apology for having been in love with Bramber's wife, albeit years ago. But there was nothing that pointed to Torrance wanting harm to come to Bryony Sandwell. Far from it, he seemed genuinely concerned about her. More than that, he came across as a caring lad, although Cooper knew how clever criminals were when it came to disguising the truth.

The brief time he'd spent with Miss Sandwell in the hospital the previous afternoon had proved equally unhelpful. She couldn't think of a reason why anyone would want to hurt her. She certainly didn't appear to be the kind of person who would attract enemies. Although Cooper knew it was dangerous to make assumptions about anyone. One thing that did strike him as odd was the moment he was about to leave. She grabbed hold of his hand. 'You'll tell me when you find John, won't you?' she said. Clearly a plea, but not one he could pigeonhole. Was it based on a hope that Bramber would be found safely, or that once Bramber's body was discovered the trail might lead to her? The cleverest of criminals were often the ones who wanted to be found out, to be complimented for the intricacy of their crimes. A dreadful thought, but could it be that Miss Sandwell had tinkered with her own brakes, imagining it would put someone else into the frame, thereby proving herself innocent?

The team were ready and waiting, each of them looking up as he walked in. They were a good bunch, as keen to get a result as he was. But this was turning out to be a frustrating case. Almost two days had passed since the call came in about John Bramber's disappearance and since then no real leads. With Bryony Sandwell's crash happening so soon afterwards Cooper felt a sense of unease. Bramber came from a world of business, where money could easily lead to a crime. But the young woman came from the opposite end of the spectrum. She had little or nothing. What was the connection between them? If Cooper could establish that perhaps he would be one step closer to solving both crimes.

'Armstrong, what have you got for us? Any closer to finding out about this Old Tommy character?' Cooper stood at the front of the room, a felt-tip pen in his hand, ready to add something to the information board.

'Yes and no, sir. I've spoken to Old Tommy. It's a pretty sad case. I eventually found him in a bedsit. It was awfully bleak, sir. All four walls running with damp, wallpaper bubbling up with mould, and the wooden windowsill so rotten I could have put a finger straight through it. Old Tommy answered the door, but as soon as I walked in he stumbled back onto his bed, as if he could barely stand. Several empty whisky bottles lay on the floor, beside an enamel plate with a half-eaten pork pie on it. He was in a bad way, sir.'

'Drunk?'

'Very. So much so he could barely string a sentence together, at least nothing that was comprehensible. I asked him about the betting shop incident. I mentioned Bramber, but he said he couldn't remember any of it. To be honest, I think he drinks his way through the day, hoping the alcohol will lead to some sort of oblivion.'

Cooper could see that Armstrong had been moved by what he had seen and heard, perhaps the young sergeant's first glimpse into the seedier side of life in Brighton.

'I'm guessing this makes you think he can't be our man? That he wouldn't be able to stand upright long enough to get himself out to the university, to chase down Bramber. And certainly no connection you could establish with Bryony Sandwell?'

'No, sir. None at all.'

'Looks like we're back to square one, doesn't it? Do we think it's worth looking again at the betting shop staff? What about if we go through the accounts for each of the three shops? If we can establish someone is on the fiddle, could that give us our motive?' Cooper walked towards Kenny Fulbright, who until now had been fiddling with two paperclips, bending and unbending them. 'Kenny, I asked you to touch base with Bramber senior. Anything come out of that?'

Fulbright dropped the paperclips and opened his notebook. 'Not a pleasant man.'

'I'm not interested in whether you want to be friends with him, Kenny. What did he have to say about his son?' Cooper didn't hide his irritation.

'He wasn't keen on saying anything. He spoke as if we were looking to accuse his son of something, rather than helping to find him. Pretty weird actually. He said his son would turn up in his own time and if we carried on poking around his business affairs, he'd only speak to us through his solicitor.'

'So much for fatherly concern.'

'Did you get the sense that Bramber senior had something to hide?' Williams asked.

'He's made his riches through gambling, of course he has something to hide,' Cooper said. 'But do we think he has done something to harm his son? Thoughts, Kenny?'

Kenny Fulbright wasn't used to being asked for an opinion. It took him a second or two before he spoke. 'There would be other ways for him to punish his son, if he decided that's what he wanted to do. If he thought his son had let the family business down in some way he could take the betting shops away from him, show him up as a failure.'

'Okay, fair enough. Anyone have any other ideas?'

'Clem Richmond,' Armstrong said.

'Yes, what about her?'

'You asked us to check back through police records to see if she is known to the police. It seems that a year ago she was involved in a CND protest march. Some of the protesters got into a fight and Miss Richmond was among them. Uniformed police were on hand, they had to break up the fight and Miss Richmond was one of several to be given an official warning.'

'Right, yes, that makes sense. So Miss Richmond's run-in with our colleagues has left her with a decided antipathy towards us, eh? Anything else?'

'Sir.' Williams held her notebook up, by way of hailing the attention of her boss and the rest of the team. 'How about we rethink, forget about the business angle altogether? After all, the two incidents happened at or near to the university. Shouldn't we be focusing on the debating group? There must be a connection between John Bramber and Bryony Sandwell that has led to them both being targeted. There are four other members of that group who know each other. I reckon that's where we should be looking.'

'Okay, what do the rest of you think? Anyone in agreement with Williams?'

Armstrong was the first to respond. 'Pippa is right. Our focus has to be that group. We need to push them hard, not be fobbed off.'

'Sir, we have two people on the inside who could prove useful. Mrs Juke and Miss Frobisher have already offered to help. There's a chance some of the others will open up to them, more than they would to us.'

'I like your thinking, Williams. No harm in pursuing that as an angle, no harm at all.' Cooper said. 'Which means we should keep the group together for a while yet. Once they've disbanded, we've lost our chance. Let's you and I head back to Falmer and catch them before they disappear.'

Cooper moved towards the entrance to his own office, signalling the meeting was over for the moment. But Kenny Fulbright had other plans. Still feeling confident from his earlier exchange with his boss he stood up. 'There is another angle we could pursue.'

All eyes turned towards him, causing him to sit and pause before continuing.

'And that is...?' Cooper tossed the question towards Fulbright without looking at him.

'Mrs Blyth.'

'You'd better make your point, Fulbright. We've already said we're going back to question the group again, and that would include the evasive Mrs Blyth.'

'Another angle you said, sir. Mrs Blyth's husband has established business dealings with Mr Bramber. Maybe she knows more about that than she is saying. And she could be the connection.'

'I see what Kenny is driving at,' Williams said. 'You're thinking that Olivia Blythe could be the person who connects John Bramber and Bryony Sandwell.'

'Fine, yes. It's worth a look.' Cooper may have been grateful for Kenny's intervention, equally he may have been annoyed by it. It was an angle Cooper had already considered, although he hadn't voiced it. Now, if he said as much, it would look as though he was merely taking credit for Fulbright's ideas. He chose to say no more, leaving Williams to gather up her notebook and bag and follow him out of the station.

CHAPTER 26

IT TOOK SOME PERSUASION to convince Will to revisit Helena and more encouragement still for him to agree to Janie and Libby accompanying him.

'You don't have to come inside if you'd rather not,' Janie said.

'I'll decide when I get there,' was Will's immediate response, offering little more by way of explanation.

They had left the university not knowing if the others were going to hang around or if they were determined to return home. Earlier Olivia had made another unsuccessful attempt at contacting her husband, but seemed loath to take up the offer of a lift from Clem.

A spring shower had appeared from nowhere, stopping almost as soon as it started, but leaving a gloomy sky that matched Janie's mood. It was as if she was attached to a piece of elastic that first pulled her in the direction of home, only to tug her back towards Falmer. With the slow drip feed of information she had managed to extricate, mostly from Alison, she was beginning to form a picture. The centre of that picture focused on a time, six or seven years ago, when the group were all at school together. An event back then was still resonating through to the present day. She was sure of it.

Clem and Olivia weren't prepared to share anything with Janie or Libby. Clem had clearly developed an antipathy towards them, resentful of their interference. Whether that was a useful excuse, a way of covering up something more menacing, was impossible to tell. Olivia was more difficult to read. Much of her behaviour appeared to be no more than an act. But beneath the bravado it was clear that Olivia was fragile. She had admitted to being lonely, but beyond that there didn't seem to be anything in her character that might lead her to commit such violent acts.

Janie was hoping to clarify the picture by persuading Will to introduce them to Helena. She was all part of the same school-day crowd. Surely she could offer some insight into their teenage friendships, something that might suggest the reasons for recent events.

Will had been quiet for the journey, as had Libby. Janie had offered to drive, with Libby remaining resolute she would never drive again. With silence from the passengers the incessant squeak of the windscreen wipers created a rhythm of its own. But as they reached the edge of Barcombe Woods, the rain eased and then stopped completely, allowing Janie to turn off the wipers.

'Thank goodness,' she said, more to herself than to her companions in the car. 'That noise was driving me nuts. Libby, when we're home make sure you buy some new wiper blades, these are so worn they're barely doing the job they're supposed to.'

Their warm breath conflicted with the damp air outside, causing the windows to mist up. Janie wound her window down a little. Perhaps it was the fresh air wafting through the car that sparked her passengers into conversation because the next moment they both went to speak at once.

'You grew up round here?' was Libby's offering, while at the same time Will said, 'We've just passed my old house.'

They fell into silence again as they travelled down Sayers Lane and on towards the Bramber house, gradually weaving their way through the modern estate.

'Crikey, so this is what rich looks like, is it?' Libby said.

Each house they passed was individually designed, some with fancy porticos, suggesting Roman or Greek architecture, others modelled on a Tudor style, with decorative black timbers on a white frontage. Professionally landscaped front gardens boasted blooms of every colour, manicured lawns, and neatly edged pathways.

'I wouldn't give you a thank you for any of them,' Will said. 'These are houses, not homes. Not in my book.'

'You have to admire the design though, some of these are really stunning. Imagine what they're like inside,' Libby said.

'You won't have to imagine for long, this is it. John's house.' Will pointed to the property at the far end of the cul-de-sac, leaving Janie to pull up onto the wide driveway in front of the double garage.

'She might not even be in,' Will said.

'You sound as if you hope she won't be.' Libby looked up at the imposing frontage of the Bramber house, her injuries momentarily forgotten.

'Shall we go in on our own?' Janie switched the engine off and turned to look at Will. 'It might be easier in some ways.'

He seemed to be undecided, giving himself time to think by preparing a roll-up.

'Let's go,' Libby said, taking the initiative. 'You can always join us later.' Not waiting for a response, Libby led the way up the front path, with Janie following behind.

'We need to take it easy.' Janie laid a hand on Libby's shoulder, holding her back from ringing the doorbell. 'She doesn't know us for one thing, plus she'll still be desperate for news about John.'

Helena must have been watching them arrive as they were barely at the door when it opened and for the first time they came face-to-face with the woman who had broken Will's heart. She wore no make-up, which was unsurprising. A woman concerned about her husband was hardly likely to spend time gazing into a mirror, preening herself.

'Oh,' was her initial greeting.

It was impossible to know if her expression denoted surprise or anxiety.

'Mrs Bramber, sorry, you don't know us, but we've been at the university conference with your husband.' Janie offered studied Helena's face for a reaction. The change was imperceptible, a slight relaxing of the forehead, the beginnings of a polite smile showing off her dimples. It was easy to see why Will had fallen for this beauty, who even now could have graced the front cover of any magazine.

'You'd best come in.' Helena led the way along the wide corridor into the open plan living area. It was several moments before anyone spoke. Libby's focus was on the interior design, the striking colours, furniture she had only ever seen in magazines. Janie, on the other hand, noticed the two empty coffee cups.

'This isn't a good time for me,' Helena said, looking down at the coffee cups, but making no move to clear them away. 'I'm not sure why you've come or how you found me.'

'Sorry,' Janie said. 'We should have explained. Will is here with us. He's in the car.'

'Will?'

Janie could see conflicted emotions in Helena's expression, but surely that shouldn't be a surprise. Here was a woman whose husband had suddenly disappeared, whose car had been found run into a tree. Hours later an old flame turns up, someone she hadn't seen for years, and now two complete strangers were standing in her living room.

'Mrs Bramber, Helena,' Janie began. 'We only want to help. You were at school with the others in the group; Olivia, Alison, and Clem. You all knew John and Will from back then. Bryony too.'

The merest flicker of panic crossed Helena's eyes, panic she seemed able to quickly control.

'Bryony?'

'Bryony Sandwell. The police may not have mentioned it to you, but Bryony had a terrible accident yesterday. She was at the conference with us, with John. We know you were all at school together. So, we were just thinking, with Bryony being targeted so soon after John's disappearance, somehow the two things might be connected. Maybe the connection relates to years back, when you were all friends.' Janie's words tailed off. Shooting in the dark, is what I'm doing.

'We weren't all friends.'

Helena's pronouncement confirmed what Alison had told them. For different reasons Olivia and Bryony had been kept on the outside, but Alison hadn't made clear how Helena fitted into the friendship group. Did she also hold a fascination for Clem's forthright opinions, or was it only John and Will's love for Helena that created a tenuous link to the others?

'Is Bryony alright?' There was an edge to Helena's question that Janie couldn't pinhole.

'She was lucky. The crash could have killed her.' Libby still struggled to hold her emotions in check each time she had to revisit the event. 'I was there. I was the one who pulled her out of the wreckage.'

'That was a brave thing to do,' Helena said. 'Were you injured too?'

The long-sleeved blouse continued to hide the worst of Libby's injuries, leaving only the two plasters across the back of her right hand in view.

'A few scrapes, that's all. Helena, do you have any idea who might want to hurt your husband, or Bryony? Did anything happen back then, when you were all teenagers? Someone who might still be holding a grudge?'

Helena moved over to the long sofa beside the French windows and sat, gesturing to Libby and Janie to do the same. The light from outside was more grey than bright, throwing a dappled shadow across the room. The backdrop to the sofa was a full height painting; abstract art. Thick bands of purple, yellow, and orange, providing a stark contrast to the simplicity of Helena's dress, grey shot silk that shimmered as she moved.

'You're looking in the wrong place,' Helena said at last.

'Where should we be looking?' Janie asked.

'Trust me, it's best you don't get involved.'

They had only been in Helena's presence for about ten minutes, during which time she had looked at her wristwatch repeatedly and now she glanced down at it again.

'Do you have to be somewhere? Perhaps we're holding you up?' Janie asked.

Helena shook her head and looked towards the French windows. 'I can't help you,' she said at last.

'Can't, or won't? Surely you want to know what's happened to your husband. If there's something, anything, you can tell us...' Even as she spoke Janie guessed she was unlikely to receive a useful response.

'I'd like you to go now.' Helena stood, walked to the doorway and waited for them.

'We won't give up, Helena. We'll keep doing what we can to help bring John back safely to you,' Janie said once she reached the front door.

'Like I said, you're wasting your time.'Moments later they were back in the car, with Helena standing in her doorway watching as Janie pulled out of the drive.

'That went well,' Janie said. There was no disguising her disappointment.

'She couldn't help?' Will asked, turning to watch from the rear window as Helena stepped back into the house.

'For some unaccountable reason she didn't want to help.'

'She must be as mystified as we are. Worse though. It's her husband who's vanished, remember.'

'It's more than that. She practically warned us off.' Janie was still determining the implications of what Helena had said, as well as her reactions.

She turned the engine on, looking in the rear-view mirror before pulling away. As she did, she noticed Will was still gazing out of the back window. With his attention elsewhere she whispered to Libby. 'Did you see the bruise?'

'What bruise?' Libby said.

'The one on her wrist beside her watch. She kept looking at it, I reckon it was really hurting her.'

'You think it could be relevant?'

'It could be something, it could be nothing. But I've got a hunch and now we have to hope for something to fall into our laps that will prove it's right.'

CHAPTER 27

DETECTIVE INSPECTOR COOPER AND WPC Williams were en route to Falmer when the call came in on the radio.

'They've found a body, sir.' It was Armstrong who had taken the report. The phone call came in just after one 'o'clock from someone who refused to give a name.

'What do we know, Armstrong? Is it Bramber?'

'Nothing confirmed, sir. An anonymous caller saying he's spotted a body at the foot of Ditchling Beacon. Uniform are on the scene. Shall I attend?'

'We'll head there now. We're fifteen minutes away at most.'

As one of the highest points of the South Downs, Ditchling Beacon was a popular area for ramblers and picnickers. Just a few miles north of Brighton it provided a welcome contrast to the noisy and populated town. Once an Iron Age hill fort the northern face of the Beacon was the steepest, offering views across the South Downs in all directions. The only road access to the summit was via the steep and narrow Beacon Road. There had been plenty of road accidents over the years, several where victims had suffered life-changing injuries, others where they had lost their lives. The turn off from Sayers Lane into Beacon Road had recently been designated an accident black spot. But as far as Cooper knew, no rambler had ever lost his life by falling from the Beacon itself.

As Cooper negotiated the final stretch of Beacon Road, he saw two police cars and an ambulance ahead of him. Parking up on the grassy bank beside the road, he got out of the car, with Williams following close behind.

'What have we got?' he asked the young police constable who approached him. 'Body hasn't been moved, I hope?'

'No, sir. White male, mid-twenties, well dressed. The pathologist thinks death is as a result of a broken neck.'

It was a short but steep climb down the slope to join Max Admiral, the police pathologist. Cooper had worked with Max over several years and had grown used to his monosyllabic manner. A forensic focus on the job in hand usually meant Max had little patience for inane questions or casual conversation.

'Max,' Cooper nodded a greeting.

'Fracture of the upper cervical. More after the post-mortem.'

'Anything that would provide identification?'

Max turned to the uniformed constable. 'You may check his pockets, constable. Don't disturb anything else, the photographer still needs to do his work.'

The man's body was on his right side, both legs bent, and both arms outstretched. Cooper's guess was it wasn't only the man's neck that was broken, at least one or more of his limbs had suffered in the fall. Cooper stood close to the body and looked back up the hill towards the car park, imagining how the incident might have occurred. The ground underfoot was slippery as a result of the sharp rain shower from earlier.

'A fall, or suicide?' he asked Max.

'As I said. More after the post-mortem.'

The uniformed constable finished checking the man's four pockets, two in his jacket, two in his trousers.

'Nothing here, sir.'

'No wallet?'

'No sir.'

If this was John Bramber, it wouldn't be surprising there was no wallet. His wallet had been found in Barcombe Woods. What could have happened here? When the crash in the woods didn't kill him has he been brought here to finish him off?

'The photo, Williams.' Cooper turned to his constable, who was entirely focused on the scene, her eyes scouring the surrounding area.

She slipped her hand into her top pocket, taking out a small black-and-white photograph. As they were leaving the Bramber house the day before, Cooper had asked Helena Bramber for a photo of her husband. It was only when she left the room to fetch the snapshot that he noticed there were no framed photographs on display of the two of them. Not necessarily unusual, some folk chose not to look at photos of themselves. In truth he could only think of one in his own living room, taken on his wedding day. Mrs Bramber handed over the photo with an apology. 'It's the only one I can lay my hands on just now, will it do?'

At the time Cooper had hoped he wouldn't need it, that John Bramber would turn up of his own accord. But now, looking at the body lying a short distance away, he was annoyed with himself. The print had been produced from one of those self-service photo booths and was grainy at best. Helena Bramber said it had been taken some years ago. 'When he had long hair,' she offered as an explanation. Cooper guessed the younger man's hairstyle was fashioned on some of the rock and pop bands that had come to the fore over recent times. Noise without melody had been Cooper's reaction to it when he'd heard the music. Give me Mozart any day.

Max was kneeling beside the body when Cooper passed the photo to him.

'Your thoughts, Max? Is it him? The chap in this photo has been missing since Thursday evening. He lives in the vicinity. Have I got to break the bad news to his wife?'

Max removed his wire-rimmed glasses and studied the photo. Then with precision he moved the body slightly to get a clearer look at his face. As he did so Cooper noticed how one side of the man's face was covered with blood, possibly from a wide gash across his temple. The black-and-white photo gave few clues, except that John Bramber had dark hair, as did the victim lying in front of him.

'Can't say for definite,' Max said, handing the photo back. 'Next of kin will have to identify. If you'll leave me to do what I need to do...'

'When will you have something for me?'

'5pm.'

'Now for the worst part of this job,' Cooper said, turning to Williams. Retracing their steps they returned to the car. Cooper radioed in and spoke to Armstrong, confirming that for now they would treat the death as suspicious.

'We'll advise Mrs Bramber of the situation and ask her if she can identify the body.'

'Yes, sir. Does that mean the case is closed?' Armstrong said.

'Forgotten Mrs Sandwell, have you, eh? It's far from closed, I'd say. Even if Bramber's fall was an accident, we have to establish how he got from Barcombe Woods to Ditchling Beacon without his car. Bit too far to walk, don't you think?'

'Yes, sir. Should I continue to see what else I can uncover regarding Mr Bramber's business dealings?'

'Take a closer look at Roger Blyth. We know the two had business connections. If you can establish the detail, it could prove useful.'

The ten minute drive to the Bramber home didn't offer Cooper much time to think through his approach. His own mantra of never making assumptions was at the forefront of his mind after this latest discovery. The body of a man had been found, matching the description of John Bramber in terms of age, hair colour, but little more than that. He needed to prepare the man's wife for the very worse news, that her husband was dead, while maintaining the possibility the body wasn't John Bramber. And if not John, then who? That would leave Cooper with a suspicious death to investigate, while knowing little or nothing about the victim. More than that, if this wasn't John Bramber's body, where was the betting shop owner? Was there another body yet to be discovered?

As Cooper pulled the car up onto the drive of the Bramber house, he noticed the merest of movements in the voile curtain that hung at the front bay window. A moment later Helena Bramber was coming towards him, both hands clinging tightly to the fine woollen shawl wrapped around her shoulders.

'You have news?' She asked in such a way that Cooper guessed she wanted the answer to be in the negative. The old saying of no news being good news could never be truer at this moment.

'Shall we go inside?' Cooper stood back, allowing Helena to walk slowly into the house. Williams kept a few paces behind him, closing the door once they were all in the hall. There was a moment's hesitation when Helena seemed unsure whether to move into the living room, or remain in the hallway. How do you choose where to be when you fear you are about to hear the worst possible news, news that will stay with you forever?

'Let's all sit down, eh?' Cooper stepped in front of Helena, taking the decision from her, leading them all to the living room. He and Williams sat side-by-side on one sofa, while Helena stood by the French windows, her back turned towards them.

'You've found him?' she said. A statement of fact expecting only confirmation.

'Mrs Bramber, we've found the body of a man up at Ditchling Beacon.'

Williams told Armstrong later that as she watched Helena fall to the floor, it was like watching one of those wooden puppets she had played with as a child. As the strings were let go, the legs would fold up beneath the puppet, as if the life had gone out of them.

Without asking, Cooper went through to the kitchen and poured a glass of water. By the time she came back through Williams had helped Helena up to sitting, propped up against the armchair.

'Here, take a sip.'

Helena took the glass with one hand, using the other to steady the shaking.

'Take your time.' Cooper said, waiting for the moment when he felt Helena could hear the next piece of information he needed to share with her.

After a few sips of the water she put the glass on the side table and stood, smoothing down her dress as if in doing so she was smoothing down her emotions.

'The thing is, Mrs Bramber. We can't be certain whether the body we have found is your husband. The photo you gave us...'

'You need me to identify him?'

Cooper nodded, wondering whether there would ever come a day when asking such a request of a grieving relative wouldn't turn his stomach.

'When you're ready.'

It was a dilemma. He would like to give Helena Bramber time, to recover from the shock of the news he had to convey, time to prepare herself for what might be the final goodbye to her husband. But any delay was a delay to the investigation. He wanted answers and he wanted them now.

'I'll never be ready,' she said at last, moving towards the doorway.

As they followed her outside, Cooper noticed a man from a nearby property mowing his lawn.

'At least it's not a police car,' Helena said, nodding to the neighbour. 'There'd be news of an arrest flying around the estate in no time. Not something they'd ever accept.' She gave a muted laugh. 'Oh dear me, no. A criminal in their midst, whatever next.'

'Not the friendliest of communities?' Cooper asked.

'Not a community, Detective Inspector. A bunch of people who think they've made it, who think wealth beats everything.'

There was no disguising the bitterness in her tone.

During the ten minute drive to the police station Cooper prepared a mental list of tasks. Once the body had been identified and Max had determined if death was as a result of an accident, suicide, or something more sinister, Cooper would need to bring his team together. Max's verdict from the post-mortem would dictate the route for the investigation. If John Bramber had accidentally fallen to his death, there was still the matter of how he'd got to Ditchling Beacon without his car. The same went for suicide, although the question then would be what might have brought Bramber to such depths as to cause him to take his own life. From what the members of the debating group had said there was nothing in his manner on that Thursday evening to indicate he was depressed or worried. The third possibility, that someone else had been present, causing the man's death, would require the team to dig deeper. Who and why? Surely motive was the key. At the same time, someone had caused Miss Sandwell's crash. The same person? Or was the timing of the two events nothing more than a coincidence?

He parked in his usual spot. Williams knew the drill. Recently they had worked together on another case. A vagrant had been found dead in one of the alleyways in central Brighton. Williams had tracked down another homeless man, who offered to do the identification. Her manner throughout was perfect, calm, non-judgemental. Just what would be needed again.

Cooper walked behind as Williams led Helena towards the mortuary, showing her into a small glass-fronted room from where she could view the body.

'I'm sorry but I think I'm going to be sick.' Helena said in such an apologetic tone Cooper wished he could stop the process there and then.

'It's fine, really,' Williams said, easing Helena into a chair. 'There's no rush, just take your time. Here have some water.' She passed Helena a paper cup which she had filled from a water dispenser. She took a few sips, then handed it back to the constable.

'Thank you. I'm okay now. You can go ahead.'

The mortuary attendant was standing beside the body, which was laid out on a table, covered with a white sheet. As Cooper nodded to him he pulled the sheet back to reveal the man's face.

'No, dear God, no,' were Helena's words, as once again her legs folded beneath her and she fell to the floor.

Williams was beside her immediately, her hand on her shoulder and after a moment an arm helping her to stand.

'I'm so sorry, Mrs Bramber,' Cooper said. 'But we need you to confirm... this is your husband, Mr John Bramber?'

'John? No, this isn't John. It's not my husband.'

CHAPTER 28

Had Janie known about the events taking place in and around Ditchling Beacon she might have approached her visit to the hospital in a different frame of mind.

She'd decided to visit Bryony on her own, for which Libby was grateful. The shock of witnessing Bryony's crash was still replaying in Libby's mind and seeing the vulnerability of the young woman lying in the hospital bed only made it worse.

The same ward sister was on duty when Janie reached the ward. On their previous visit Libby had been allowed in to speak to Bryony, leaving Janie in the corridor. She kept her fingers crossed behind her back as she approached the ward sister, who was at the nursing station speaking to a junior nurse. Janie waited for a break in their conversation.

'Is it possible to visit Miss Sandwell?'

'And you are?' The ward sister's steely glare left Janie feeling like an awkward schoolgirl.

'A friend. I was here yesterday with another of Miss Sandwell's friends. The one who was present at the scene of the accident.' She wondered how much more she would have to say and whether any of it would make a difference to the outcome.

'A short visit and the patient is absolutely not to be upset. We had the police here, asking the poor girl all sorts. She needs rest, not interrogation.'

Janie wasn't sure whether the accusation was a warning, or merely a comment, so she refrained from responding and waited.

'In you go. Ten minutes at most.'

As she walked towards Bryony's bed she realised she hadn't brought anything with her. Grapes, flowers, a magazine, something that might bring a moment's cheer. But then, looking at Bryony, who was lying very still, her eyes closed, her skin almost as pale as the bedsheet, Janie reflected that the thing most likely to bring cheer would be to discover why Bryony had been targeted and then to bring the perpetrator to justice.

'Bryony, hello. It's Janie. I've only come to see how you're doing.'

Bryony opened her eyes, looking towards Janie while keeping her head still on the pillow. As if even that was uncomfortable, she closed her eyes again.

'Thank you for coming. But do you mind if I don't look at you? My head still hurts so much.'

'Libby says hello.'

'Libby, yes. Was she badly hurt? She was so brave pulling me from the car. I can't remember all of it, just bits and pieces, flashbacks. I was so scared, Janie.'

'Libby is fine, you mustn't worry about her. Your job is to concentrate on getting better.'

Janie reflected that Bryony might be the only person willing or able to answer the questions that needed to be answered, but was this really the right time? Perhaps she should wait until Bryony was feeling stronger, out of danger. And yet, if Janie's theory was right, getting answers now might prevent another tragedy.

'All my life I've made bad decisions.' It seemed there would be no need to ask questions, all Janie needed to do was listen.

'I reckon my parents knew I would be a bad'un, that's why they got rid of me,' Bryony continued. 'You see, I grew up in care, three different children's homes, each one as soul-destroying as the last. But school was different, it offered a world where I could be someone else. In term time I used to long for Monday mornings. Maybe if I'd stayed at Longley Comp things would have turned out differently.'

'Longley Comp?'

'The first secondary school I went to. I was doing so well, top of the class in most subjects, but then I was accused of stealing. I wasn't guilty and I knew who'd done it, but I had no way of proving it. So when they found the money in my locker, I was out on my ear. The couple who ran the care home stood up for me, I'll give them that. They said I'd never done anything like that before and that I should be given a second chance. But the school head decided I couldn't stay there so they transferred me to Ringwood.'

'The same school as Clem and Alison.'

'From the very first day I hated it. I didn't know anyone there. What friends I had were back in Longley Comp. So in lunch-break I used to sit on my own in the playground. But then I started to listen to Clem. She used to give these speeches; there was always a crowd gathered around her. She was inspiring, making us think we had the power to be whoever we wanted to be. I'd never heard anyone speak about those things before.'

'You wanted to know more?'

'I used to hang around her, asking questions, trying to understand. I suppose I was pretty annoying.'

Bryony stopped speaking and Janie got the impression she was revisiting that time, struggling to unravel how the hopeful teenager she had been back then had become the woman she was now; uncertain, guilt laden.

Then Bryony continued. 'John and Will used to sit on the wall outside our school. They were there most afternoons when we came out. Of course, they barely knew I existed.'

'That's when Will met Helena?'

'Will and Helena, yes. It was stupid really, but I set myself a challenge, like a dare. I suppose I thought if I could get John to notice me, I'd get the attention of Clem. Make her jealous.'

'Clem and John?' This wasn't something Janie had expected to hear.

'Clem, Olivia, even Alison. They all had eyes for John. Clem in particular, she was besotted. The more he ignored her the more she wanted him.'

'Did he know?'

'Oh, he knew alright. It was a power play for him. A game. And I was crazy enough to believe I could lure him in, make Clem believe I was someone to be recognised. That if John noticed me, well then...'

Janie guessed how this had played out, but wanted Bryony to explain in her own words.

'I pretty much handed myself to John on a plate. I suppose he couldn't believe his luck.'

'And you were fourteen?'

'Fifteen by the time I discovered I was pregnant.'

'Dear God, Bryony, you poor thing. And John was the father?'

'Oh, he denied it. Told me I was a silly little girl and if I told anyone he was the father they'd never believe me. "Come on, who'd imagine I'd want you when I can have any girl I choose?" is what he said.'

'Did you tell anyone?'

Bryony went to shake her head, but stopped herself, opening her eyes instead. 'He was right, of course. No one would believe me. I'd already been labelled a liar from the stealing episode and you know what they say, no smoke without fire. But three months in and there was no hiding it. The couple in charge of the home arranged for me to go somewhere to have the baby.'

'You had to leave school?'

'I never told the others why I was leaving, but I'm sure they guessed.'

'And your baby?'

'A daughter. I had just six weeks with her and then she was taken from me.'

'Oh Bryony, I can't imagine how painful that must have been for you.' In fact Janie could imagine it, perhaps too well. And right now she wished she could be transported home to her own daughter, to hold her tight and never let her go.

'I gave birth in a mother and baby home and the woman who ran the place arranged the adoption. It was truly a bleak time for all of us girls. When prospective parents turned up, they kept us out of the way, told us to stay in our rooms. So we knew that would be a day when someone would lose their child forever. There was a camaraderie of sorts among us. We'd support each other, knowing eventually it would be our turn to have our heart broken. One girl attempted suicide the day after they took her little boy. Another ran away, perhaps she thought she could find her little one. Who knows? But, yes, the day finally came when it was my turn. I wasn't allowed to say goodbye to her and I've no idea where she is now. I called her Rose, but they might have changed her name, who knows? What goes around, comes around, I suppose? My parents dumped me and my daughter probably thinks I dumped her. More than anything I wish I could have kept her. I would have made sure I was the best mother any child could wish for.'

Janie was struggling to keep the tears from falling. As she listened to what Bryony had had to endure it was as if she was going through it alongside her.

'And John?'

'He got off scot-free. Married Helena, went on to have a great life.'

'And it was John who suggested you come along this weekend?'

'Since the day they took my little girl from me I've vowed I'd confront him. But it's taken me until now to summon up the courage. It wasn't difficult to track him down. I wrote to him via one of his betting shops, keeping the letter light-hearted. Telling him it was all water under the bridge, old hurts forgotten. I said it would be good to see him and he wrote back and told me about this weekend. But I'm not stupid, I know now it was all a game for him. He'd thought he'd have a laugh at my expense, knowing the others would all be here, knowing I'd struggle with that.'

'And Thursday was the first time you'd seen him since you'd had your daughter?'

'I'm not sure what I expected to feel. Anger, sadness, regret? On first sight, maybe all of those. He hasn't really changed at all, still oozing confidence. I suppose that's what comes from having a wealthy family behind you.' She hesitated, then continued. 'Anyway, I waited until we had the break before supper and I followed him outside.'

'And you saw him get into his car?'

'He was standing beside his car. That was the moment I knew I had to say something. I hadn't really planned any of it, but at that moment I wanted to make him see what he'd done, how he'd help to destroy my life. I guess I was hoping for an apology, or at least some sign of remorse.'

'You confronted him?'

'I told him I'd let everyone know the truth. I'll make your life as miserable as you've made mine, is what I said. He just laughed. Told me I had no proof. "People will think you're a pathetic woman still desperate to be in with the crowd. They don't want you, can't you see that? And I don't want you, I never have." Those were his words. He held all the cards. I had nothing. That's how he's always made feel, like nothing.'

'So cruel,' Janie said, under her breath. She wondered what Libby would say when she heard the truth about John Bramber.

'He started to get into his car. And that's when I realised I had one ace. I shouted at him, told him I'd tell his wife, his precious Helena. That got his attention. He moved towards me. That's when I reminded him about his birthmark. It's high on his inner thigh, near his groin. It's not likely someone would know about it unless they've seen it at close quarters, so to speak. And that's when he went crazy. He grabbed me by the shoulders and shook me so hard. I thought he was going to hit me. Then, suddenly he let go. We stood there, facing each other and then he said, "Do your worst if you think it will get you anywhere. But something tells me you'll be the loser. Again. You see, John Bramber always wins."'

Janie wasn't certain if the police had told Bryony about the true cause of her car crash. But it was pretty clear to her now who had cut the brake pipe and why. John Bramber intended it as a warning to Bryony, or worse still, he had hoped to shut her up for good.

'And you saw him get into his car and drive away?'

'No, I left him standing there in the car park, but I guess he left soon afterwards. And then he didn't come back that evening.' She paused and at first Janie wondered if she had no energy left to continue her account. But then she said, 'I knocked on your bedroom door Thursday night.'

'It was you? Libby thought she'd heard someone.'

'You both seemed so kind. I guessed you'd both be understanding. I wanted to tell you about John, about the argument, but then I lost my nerve. You probably think the same as the others, that everything that's happened is my own fault. It's what I think too.'

'Oh no, Bryony. We don't think that at all. You were brave to confront John like that. It's such a shame you weren't able to confide in us.'

Janie's fleeting thought was what may have been avoided if only Bryony had knocked harder on the door, if she had been able to share her fears about John, about his anger and accusations. Could the trauma and injuries Bryony was now suffering have been averted?

'Anyway, I thought about it all during the night. And the next day I decided to make good on my promise. I was on my way to speak to Helena Bramber, to tell her everything about John and me, when I had the accident. But it wasn't an accident, was it, Janie? John tried to kill me, didn't he?'

Her voice had become increasingly quiet, as if the process of explaining had taken the last of her energy.

'You see, I was right what I said to Libby yesterday. I'm a bad person, I deserve everything that has happened to me. If I hadn't tempted John into a relationship with me none of this would have happened. It's my fault, Janie. All of it.'

CHAPTER 29

JANIE HAD NO AGENDA in mind when she made the phone call to Detective Inspector Cooper. This wasn't about scoring points, a rush to be the first to reach a conclusion to the case. The important thing now was to flush out the perpetrator and bring him to justice.

'Detective Inspector, I've discovered something. It could help to explain John Bramber's disappearance.'

She had been put straight through to Cooper, who had just returned from the mortuary. Williams and Armstrong had been given the task of accompanying Helena Bramber home, with an instruction to stay with her. It was clear what they were waiting for.

'You'd better come into the station, there have been developments,' he said.

Shortly after the phone call Janie was sitting in Cooper's office, mentally running through all that Bryony had told her. Cooper was in the main office, speaking to another member of his team, but then he came in and shook her hand.

'Mrs Juke,' he said and sat down.

'Detective Inspector, I've just come from the hospital. I've been speaking to Bryony Sandwell and I think you'll want to hear what she has to say.'

Cooper nodded and Janie couldn't tell if he was ready to listen or if there was something he wanted to share with her first.

'Miss Sandwell. Yes, carry on,' he said at last.

'Bryony had a child when she just fifteen. John Bramber was the father.'

'Ah.'

'John rejected Bryony completely, denied all responsibility. Bryony has had a terrible life, Detective Inspector.'

'Yes.'

Janie hesitated, wondering if she was telling the detective something he already knew. Nevertheless, she continued.

'She contacted him recently, thinking she could raise the issue of the child again. John suggested she come along to the conference this weekend and that was when she decided to confront him. She threatened to expose him, to tell everyone the truth; that he'd fathered her child when she was just fifteen years old. In particular she threatened to tell his wife.'

'And in turn John Bramber threatened Miss Sandwell?'

'Yes, sir, exactly.'

'And you believe John Bramber cut the brake pipe to Miss Sandwell's car to cause her to crash, to shut her up?'

'It seems incredible he could do such a thing, but yes, that's what I think happened.'

'Mmm.' The detective pushed some of the papers on his desk to one side, as if in doing so he was clearing his thoughts. 'The thing is Mrs Juke, we've found a body up at Ditchling Beacon.'

Janie didn't know what she had expected the 'development' to be, but certainly not this.

'John Bramber?'

'No.'

The silence in the inner office was only broken by the repetitive sound of a typewriter somewhere out in the main office.

'Then who?' Janie said, struggling to make her thoughts catch up.

'Roger Blyth.' Cooper let the words fall, adding nothing by way of explanation.

'Olivia's husband? I don't understand.'

'The thing is, Mrs Juke, you've brought me the final piece of the puzzle and for that I'm extremely grateful.'

'I have?'

'Let me set the scene. Mrs Bramber has confirmed some of what I'm going to tell you. The rest is supposition, but my guess is we're as close to the truth as we can be until we have absolute confirmation.'

He pushed his chair away from the desk, swivelled round and stretched his legs out. It was a relaxed pose that belied the events he was about to recount.

'John Bramber is desperately in love with his wife, always has been. But recently he noticed her behaviour towards him changing, he becomes suspicious. He decides to lay a trap. He tells his wife he's going away for the weekend to a conference on women's rights. Ironic, eh? Late on Thursday afternoon he leaves the university, drives his car into the woods and runs it into a tree.'

'On purpose?'

'On purpose, yes. He's got a bicycle in the back of his car and he uses that to cycle home, while first having dropped his empty wallet in the woods.'

'He wants people to believe he's had an accident, that's he's the victim of an assault, a robbery?'

'Absolutely. Because if they're worried about him they're not likely to be worrying about his planned victim.'

'Roger Blyth?'

'We think he must have a hiding place somewhere. Maybe he stayed with his parents on some pretext or other, who knows? He chose to wait until the next day before making his move. He waited until he was certain to catch Mr Blythe and his wife together. We haven't been able to get much sense from Mrs Bramber as yet, so we don't know the detail, but we do know there was a violent tussle.'

'The bruise on Helena's wrist?'

'Observant, as well as intuitive. I congratulate you, Mrs Juke, if that doesn't sound too patronising.'

Cooper was in his stride now, grateful perhaps, not only to have a receptive audience, but more importantly to be reaching the conclusion of a challenging investigation.

'But John's car is in the woods. How did he get Roger to Ditchling Beacon?'

'One of Mr Bramber's cars is in the woods. You will have noticed he has a double garage. One car for him, one for his wife. We imagine he bundled Mr Blythe into his wife's car and drove him up to the Beacon. We can't be certain if he intended to kill him, or just scare him. The post-mortem shows there were several bruises to the torso, more likely from heavy punches than from the fall, but it was the fall that killed him. Broken neck.'

It was only as the detective paused that Janie realised she had been holding her breath. Even now it seemed unimaginable that someone would choose to take the life of another person.

'So much hatred,' she said.

'Oh, no, Mrs Juke, not hatred. You've been considering possible motives, as have I. Money, dodgy business dealings, social inequalities and spirited dedication to political causes. But there is one notable omission in our list of possibilities. Love. The passionate feelings of a man for his wife.'

'And he was prepared for Bryony to die? To shut her up?'

'To protect his relationship. Yes, of course.'

'It's hardly love, though, is it?'

'How would you describe it?'

'Ownership. Possession. Yet what marriage should really be about is men and women in partnership, in balance, which pretty much supports what Clem has been telling us.'

'I couldn't agree more.'

Cooper stood, indicating the conversation had to come to an end for the moment.

'I'm really very grateful, Mrs Juke. Miss Sandwell felt she could open up to you. We might have struggled to achieve the same level of honesty through our questioning. You've played an important role.'

'It's not over, yet, though, is it?'

'We need to find Mr Bramber and we need to find him fast. He's a desperate man, he's proved he's prepared to go to any lengths to achieve his aims.'

'You think Helena is in danger?'

'If you believe something belongs to you, the first thing you do is clear away all threats to that ownership. But if you then realise that despite all you've done it will never be truly yours, better to destroy it altogether.'

Janie's drive back to Falmer gave her time to think. Roger's death was a tragedy. She wondered how Olivia would bear the news. Roger had encouraged Olivia to go away for the weekend, giving him and Helena a chance to spend more time together, rather than snatched meetings in secret. But Olivia gave no sign she suspected her husband was having an affair. It was all so sad. Unrequited love. Will loved Helena, losing her to John. Clem, Olivia, Alison, all set their sights on John, and yet Helena was the only one for him, but in the end Helena had other ideas. She loved Roger. And then there was poor Bryony. It wasn't love that drew her to John, but the desperate hope of a teenage girl that someone would notice her, treat her as an equal.

DI Cooper had thanked her and for that Janie was grateful. Although if she hadn't been distracted by feelings of guilt she might have made the connections sooner. Her first priorities would always be her daughter and her husband and it felt wrong being away from them, but her role in resolving this case gave her a sense of validation. It was a conflict inside herself she had yet to reconcile.

She needed to phone her dad to update him, but first Libby had to be brought up to speed.

Pulling into the car park she saw Libby outside Park Village, talking to Will. She pressed the hooter to get their attention and waited for them to come across to her.

'I'm not sure where to start,' she said, getting out of the car. 'Olivia's husband is dead.'

'Dear God,' Libby said. 'How, where?'

'It's even worse than that.'

'How can it be worse?' Will said.

'It looks as though John is responsible.'

'That doesn't make any sense. John is the victim, isn't he?' Libby's confusion was mirrored in Will's expression.

'Let's go inside and I'll tell you everything.' Janie led the way into the refectory and waited until they were all seated before setting out all she had discovered over recent hours.

'And the police believe that John is alive?' Libby was struggling to keep pace with the dramatic change in events.

'He's alive alright, but if I get my hands on him he won't be for much longer. Trying to kill Bryony, and pushing Roger to his death. The man's a monster. And now they think Helena is in danger?' Will stood and moved towards the door. 'I'll have to go to her, someone needs to warn her.'

'Calm down, Will.' Janie took his arm, pulling him away from the door. 'The police have it in hand. You can't get involved.'

'I am involved. We all are.' He sat again and put his head in his hands. 'What a mess. Poor Olivia. Do you think she had any idea about Roger and Helena?'

'It might have been easier if they were all still here. At least Olivia wouldn't have been on her own when she's given the terrible news.'

'They left soon after you went to visit Bryony,' Libby said. 'Alison came to say goodbye and gave me their addresses in case we wanted to keep in touch.' She took a slip of paper from her waistcoat pocket and handed it to Janie. 'I wonder if Clem and Alison will support Olivia once they discover what's happened. They say charity begins at home. It's a shame Clem can't put as much effort into supporting her friends as she does fighting for women's rights. There we were, thinking we'd have a few relaxing days away from home, enjoying intelligent conversation among like-minded people. Instead we end up meeting a murderer. And to think I imagined he and I could be friends. Shows what a hopeless judge of character I am.' She turned to Janie, who avoided her gaze. This wasn't the time for I told you so.

'What do we do now?' Will asked. 'I really need to know that Helena is okay. I can't bear the thought of anything bad happening to her. She might not be blameless, but she doesn't deserve to be punished. None of us can help who we fall in love with.'

'Are the police hoping to find John? Do they have any clues as to where he might be hiding?' Libby said.

'We've got to leave it to the police and trust them to get the right result, Will. I told DI Cooper we'd wait here at the university until we hear from him. I'm confident we'll have news by this evening.'

'Good news, I hope,' Libby said. 'I can't bear it otherwise.

CHAPTER 30

WPC WILLIAMS ALWAYS TRIED to remain objective when it came to work. Emotion muddied the waters. Even so, some of the cases she had worked on tested her resolve. And this was one such case. Watching Helena Bramber fall to the floor as the mortuary attendant pulled back the sheet would have challenged anyone to remain unemotional. The tension in the little side room was palpable. There was no knowing whether Helena anticipated the dead body would be that of her lover. Just as she was preparing herself for the worst news, perhaps she also held out a slender hope that it was her husband who had died. That Roger Blythe had succeeded in the struggle that must have occurred somewhere near the top of Ditchling Beacon.

The two men – John Bramber and Roger Blythe – were so similar in looks, height and colouring. They could easily have been brothers. Instead, despite being business associates, they were enemies. All for the love of one woman.

Cooper had tasked Williams and Armstrong to accompany Helena home. Williams was well aware that it was unusual for a WPC to be given as much responsibility as DI Cooper had given her. She had always made it clear that she was keen to learn and that when the time was right, she wanted to take her sergeant's exams and make the move to CIC. DI Cooper had said he would support her, he seemed to trust her judgement, although she was well aware of how much experience she had yet to gather.

This next stage of the investigation was a case in point. The two officers had been told to stay with Helena but to keep out of sight. The thinking was that at some point Bramber would return home to his wife, to claim his prize – or reclaim it – depending on one's viewpoint.

There was no conversation during the car journey to the Bramber house. This wasn't the time for casual words, not even for further interrogation. Williams could sense that Armstrong had questions, he was young, keen, desperate to understand the criminal mind. He'd been fast-tracked into CID so had spent little time on the beat. She wasn't even sure that Armstrong had been involved in a murder case, if indeed that what's this turned out to be.

The car slowed, at which point Helena went to speak.

'It's okay,' Williams said. 'We're going to park a couple of streets away. Best not to make our presence too obvious.'

It was difficult to know what Helena Bramber was thinking, what she was feeling. She must have known the police were waiting for her husband to turn up, that they were setting a trap, with her as the bait. Did she have any remaining loyalty to him? Would she try to warn him, or was she hoping he would be caught and punished for the ultimate crime – murder?

Once inside the house Williams signalled to Armstrong to do a quick recce of all the rooms. Bramber may have already arrived and be secreting himself, waiting for his wife to return.

A few minutes later Armstrong returned. 'Nothing,' he said.

'Best check the garage,' Williams said.

There was an assumption that Bramber had taken Roger Blythe to Ditchling Beacon in his wife's car. If the garage was empty Bramber could be anywhere. If he wanted to escape capture, it would be easy enough, drive north perhaps, even abroad. If that was the case, tracking him down would be nigh on impossible. But they were all banking on the assumption that Bramber wouldn't be able to walk away from his one true love – Helena. Everything he'd done up until now - planning his supposed disappearance, arranging for Bryony's accident, killing Roger Blythe – was about clearing the path to Helena. Perhaps, Williams mused, Bramber hoped that somehow, in his twisted mind, he could get her to love him again.

'I'll make coffee, shall I?' There was something so normal in Helena's tone. It was as if Williams had come into the wrong house. Not a place where another tragedy was imminent, but where friends could all sit down together for a comfortable evening.

Williams followed Helena through to the kitchen. On Williams' first visit to the house, when she had accompanied her boss, she had noticed the almost clinical appearance of the kitchen. Gleaming worktops stretched the length of one wall, with nothing on show except an electric kettle and a colourful pottery jug displaying a bunch of crimson tulips. The tulips drooped, as if they sensed the sadness of the moment.

Helena slid a tray from a narrow gap between the fitted cupboards and began to lay it out with mugs, a sugar bowl, and a cream jug, putting it onto the breakfast bar.

'Should we have biscuits?'

It was if she was in a dream state.

'Let me do that, you sit down.' Williams said. 'We don't want you falling again, do we?'

Helena perched on one of the stools, laying her hands out on the breakfast bar, inspecting them as she spoke.

'I did love him, you know.'

'Roger?'

'My husband. When we got married, I thought I was the luckiest girl alive. Everyone was in love with John Bramber and he chose me.'

Williams remained silent, looking away from Helena to give her the space to open up.

'What I wasn't prepared for was the intense jealousy. The first time he accused me was on our honeymoon. Two weeks in Palma, Majorca, in a splendid hotel that looked right over the bay. The views were indescribably beautiful.'

She gazed into the distance as if every fibre of her being wished she was back there, standing on the balcony, gazing onto the Mediterranean, with all that had happened since vanished into the ether.

'The first evening we ate in the hotel restaurant, which was set outside on the terrace. The atmosphere was relaxed, joyful. And throughout the meal a couple of local men, brothers I think, played Spanish guitar. The music was perfect, so lyrical and accomplished. Of course, I clapped along with everyone else and probably smiled at them a few times. But when we got back to our room John turned on me. He accused me of flirting and then it was as if he'd lost all sense of reality and he really hurt me.'

'He was violent towards you?'

'I passed it off as a drunken aberration. We'd both had a lot to drink.'

'But it happened again?'

Helena nodded. 'The next time he hadn't had a drink. It got so that I was scared to look at a man, or speak to anyone. And each time he was careful to inflict pain where it wouldn't show.'

She brushed her hair away from her face revealing faded bruises all around her hairline.

'And Roger?'

'He and John were business associates, but friends too, at least back then they were friends. Roger was John's best man. So Roger was often here talking through some business deal or other. I'd prepare sandwiches for them both, then stay out of the way. But before he left, Roger always sought me out, to thank me for lunch or supper. He was so kind.'

'And you became friends?'

'I knew his wife, Olivia, from school. We'd lost track of each other, which is strange because we all still live in the same area. Anyway, one Saturday morning John was making one of his regular visits to his betting shops and I had a free morning. I decided to go shopping in the Lanes and I bumped into Roger. He suggested a coffee and that was it. He was such a good listener. I guess I was ready to open up and out it all came. He was furious when he discovered how John had been treating me and I was terrified he might confront him. So I persuaded him I had it under control. I didn't, of course. But if John discovered I'd told anyone the truth about his behaviour, his rages, the unwarranted accusations, I just knew he'd want to punish me. And I was right, wasn't I?'

'How long have you and Roger been having a relationship?'

'At first it was just meeting for coffee, as and when. He made me laugh, made me feel young and free again. I'd forgotten what it was like to be happy.'

'Your friendship with Roger Blythe developed into something more?'

Helena moved to the French windows that opened out onto the back garden. Williams followed her gaze, taking in the splendour of the flower borders, the rockery set around a small fish pond. The Brambers had a life many would envy, and yet in the centre of it all was bitterness. Apparent perfection was nothing but a façade.

'Poor Roger.' Helena wrapped her arms around herself, as if trying to contain her desperation. 'And poor Olivia. We didn't mean to hurt her. If anyone is to blame, it's me. I've made one mistake after another.'

'Mrs Bramber, what was the real reason you rang the university on Friday morning? Did you have a sense your husband suspected you of having an affair?'

Helena gave the merest shrug. 'He's been behaving oddly the last few weeks, being extra nice to me. And then, out of the blue, he announces he's going to some conference at Sussex University. I suppose I rang to see if he was really there.'

'But the phone call didn't help, did it? You still weren't sure?'

'I've made such a mess of everything. You know, when I saw Will again, after so many years, I wanted to tell him, sorry. I chose the wrong man. Will and I, we could have been something special.'

The kettle had boiled once, but Williams set it to boil again. And then Armstrong came through to the kitchen.

'He's here. He's just pulled up outside.'

Armstrong looked anxious, as if uncertain as to the next move.

'We discussed this,' Williams said, hoping to engender calm in her colleague. 'I'll stay in here with Helena. You go out to meet him.'

'What if he's got a knife, or a gun?'

'We have no reason to suspect he'll be armed.'

'Let's hope we've got that right, or I won't be seeing my next birthday.'

There was no way of knowing how Helena would respond, not only to the possible threat from her husband, but to the moment when her husband's luck ran out.

Williams took Helena's arm, drawing her close beside her and raising her finger to her lips. Then it was as if they were both holding their breath as they listened for John to enter the house.

'Helena,' his call was from the hallway. 'I'm sorry about before. I'll make it up to you, I promise.'

The sound of footsteps on the parquet floor suggested John was moving along the hallway, and then into the living room, where he discovered Armstrong. 'Who the hell are you and what are you doing in my house?'

Helena tried to pull away from Williams, but the WPC just managed to stop her. They stood stock still and listened as the conversation played out in the next room.

'Detective Sergeant Armstrong, here's my warrant card.'

Williams was impressed. Armstrong's voice was calm, measured, something she was certain he wasn't feeling.

'I'll ask you again. What are you doing in my house?' Bramber said.

'I think you know that, sir.'

'What is it I'm supposed to know?'

'We've found the body of Roger Blythe up at Ditchling Beacon.'

'Roger? Well, that's sad to hear. Suicide was it?'

'What makes you say that?'

'He's been having money troubles, hoping I could bail him out. I guess he'd decided time had run out for him.'

Williams wished she could see John Bramber's expression. The calmness of his tone suggested much of this was prepared.

'Look, I'm here to speak to my wife. After all, this is my house and now you've informed me about Roger, I'd like you to leave.'

Helena must have sensed Williams had relaxed her hold, so focused was she on what was happening in the next room. Helena chose her moment and pulled away, bursting into the living room with Williams behind her.

'It's over, John,' Helena said. 'The police know. They know everything.'

'Ah, there you are, my sweetness.' John lurched towards Helena, but Armstrong barred his way. In the space of a few seconds Armstrong had somehow manhandled John Bramber to the floor. Holding him down with one knee, Williams manoeuvred Bramber's arms behind his back and handcuffed him.

'What the hell are you doing? You won't hear the last of this. I'll sue you for wrongful arrest.'

At that moment DI Cooper stepped into the room, in time to hear Bramber's outburst.

'Oh, I don't think that will happen, Mr Bramber. It seems the time has arrived for you to give up the pretence. We know about your involvement in the death of Mr Roger Blythe and about the attempted murder of Miss Bryony Sandwell.'

'Oh John, not Bryony too. Why? What can she possibly have done to you to deserve that?' Helena held her arms out towards her husband in a plea to him for the truth.

Between them Armstrong and Williams had manoeuvred Bramber into a sitting position and from there to standing. Despite the handcuffs he appeared confident, laughing in a show of bravado. 'What exactly do you think I've done?'

'We don't think you've done anything, Mr Bramber,' Cooper said. 'We know you pushed Mr Roger Blythe to his death. That's manslaughter at the very least, possibly murder. Then we have the attempted murder of Miss Bryony Sandwell. We're still awaiting the doctor's verdict, but if Miss Sandwell doesn't survive her injuries, it will be two counts of murder. How does that sound?'

Cooper scanned Bramber's face for a reaction. A few seconds passed while everyone in the room had their own expectations of what might happen next.

'You've got no proof, nothing that will stand up in court.' Bramber's voice was icily calm.

The three police officers knew he was right, there was little concrete proof to convict John Bramber. There was Bryony's admission of the fight between them, his threats. Helena had given her own account of John barging into the house late on Friday evening, forcing Roger Blythe into the car and driving away. But none of it was enough to convince a jury.

'When did you stop loving me, Helena?' At last John broke the silence. 'Was it all an act from the beginning? It was my money you really loved, wasn't it? And Roger? Did you love him? Or was he just a different meal ticket?'

'I loved you so much, but you destroyed that love with your jealousy. I couldn't breathe, John. I'd have been happy to live a simpler life, it was never about money. All this,' Helena surveyed the living room, 'it's just stuff. It means nothing. Perhaps if we'd had a child...'

'A child? Yes.' John's sudden movement towards Helena caused Armstrong to stand in front of her, protecting her from whatever her husband intended. 'She was going to tell you, that's what I couldn't allow.'

'Who was going to tell me what?'

'Bryony.'

'What about Bryony?'

'She told me I was the father of her child.'

'Oh please no, John. You and Bryony? When?'

'I really don't remember, once or twice, maybe. What difference does it make? She came on to me, what was I supposed to do, turn her down?'

'When?'

'She was always hanging around you lot, Clem, Alison, and the rest of them. Don't you remember?'

'At school? But she was in the year below us? And she left at the end of the fourth year, so, that would make her fifteen? Please don't tell me you got a fifteen-year-old pregnant?'

'Her word against mine. It might have been me, but it could just have easily been someone else, even your precious Will.'

'And Bryony threatened to tell me?'

'I couldn't have that. She had to be silenced.'

The first admission of guilt. Williams wished she could take her notebook out and write everything down, word for word, but any movement now would break the moment. She waited, anticipating Bramber's next words.

'You've destroyed that girl's life,' Helena said.

'It's not as if she had much of a life to start with, did she?'

Once the words were voiced it was as if he realised how harsh they sounded. As if perhaps for the first time in his life he was aware of how others perceived him. But there was clearly only one person whose good opinion he sought. John Bramber was still desperate for his wife to see him in a positive light, he still wanted her understanding and ultimately her love.

'And Roger? He deserved to die because he was kind to me? Because he loved me?'

'You're my wife,' John screamed the words. 'No one else has the right to love you, you're mine.'

'Oh John. You don't get it, do you? I'll never be owned. Not by you, not by anyone.'

'But you'll love me again?' The fiery anger had disappeared. His words now were of a young boy clinging tightly to the girl of his dreams.

'You have to tell the police everything, John. Admit what you've done, that you pushed Roger to his death.'

'If I tell the truth, then you'll forgive me?'

'I can never forgive you, John. But I feel sorry for you. So much destruction; Roger, Bryony, Olivia, me. And your own life. You're finished, John. It's over and I never want to see you again.'

CHAPTER 31

MAYBE THE LIGHTING OUTSIDE Falmer House wasn't working, more likely it hadn't been turned on. As the conference on women's rights was the only planned presence during the Easter break everything had been slimmed down. Reduced staff numbers in the kitchen, reduced temperature on the heating thermostats. Although somehow the dusky gloom seemed appropriate as Janie, Libby and Will sat on the wall outside the main building mulling over the news from the police station.

Will had taken the phone call confirming that DI Cooper's plan had succeeded. John Bramber had turned up at his home address and had been arrested. Beyond that little was known for certain.

'They'll be hoping for an admission of guilt,' Janie said. 'There was little or no concrete evidence to pin either crime on him.'

Will looked thoughtful as he rolled a cigarette. 'I should have realised something wasn't right. When John told me he'd suggested Bryony came this weekend, I thought it was odd. He had no time for her at school, none of them did. If I'd challenged him on it, there's a chance I might have stopped him doing what he did. If he'd suspected I was on to him at least Bryony might have been saved.'

'You can't think like that. None of this is your fault,' Janie said.

There was little appetite for a cooked supper so a plate of sandwiches and a bowl of crisps had been hastily prepared, with Mrs Blackmore expressing her disappointment the weekend had ended in such an abrupt fashion. 'Food going to waste, that's what I can't be doing with,' was her pronouncement.

They'd eaten the sandwiches in the refectory in virtual silence, before bringing the bowl of crisps outside with them. Now and then one of them stretched across and picked up a crisp.

'You know, Will,' Libby said. 'You never did play the guitar for us. I was looking forward to it.'

'Hardly the moment for it now though, is it?'

'What will you do? Is there a chance for you and Helena?'

Will gave a wry chuckle. 'I think that particular ship has sailed. That's the saying, isn't it? No, heading back to Crete. I reckon I can make a good life for myself over there. I've made a bunch of friends over the years. One of them runs a beach bar and I'm sure he'd be happy for me to help out.'

'Days on the beach, nights in a little taverna. Sounds like heaven,' Libby said, picking at the plaster on the back of her hand. 'Do you wish you'd never come back?'

'No, it's helped in a strange way. I'd hung onto a rose-tinted view of those teenage years. Now I see it for what it was, just a stepping stone from youth to manhood.'

'I guess we're all victims of events in our childhood,' Janie said, looking pensive. 'No, let me amend that, "victim" is the wrong word.'

'Do you think Olivia feels like a victim?' Libby said. 'She's certainly suffered one way or another. I wonder if she had any idea about the affair.'

'She said she felt lonely even inside her marriage,' Janie said, wondering what Will thought of Olivia when they were all teenagers, and how much she might have changed as an adult. 'I wonder if Roger's death will prove a turning point for her.'

'I'm not sure,' Libby said. 'The way I see it, our characters are pretty much mapped out from childhood and once self-doubt creeps in it's nigh on impossible to overcome.'

'I disagree.' Will stood, pacing around as if to gather his thoughts. 'I like to think that life's experiences can change us, make us stronger. I hope so anyway.'

'You're thinking about Bryony, aren't you?' Janie said.

'Yep. Her life has followed a particular course, one dreadful thing after another. But beneath it all I reckon she's tough, she could turn it around. She just needs someone to believe in her, to make her realise it's possible.'

'We'll visit her this evening, on our way home,' Janie said. 'Once she's well enough to leave hospital, we might even be able to persuade her to move to Tamarisk Bay. There are always plenty of jobs going and I could help her find a bedsit. At least she'd have us nearby to look out for her.'

'And what about you, Janie? Any clearer as to what you want?' Turning to Will she explained, 'Janie is trying to balance her responsibilities against her desires.' Then winking at Janie, she added, 'On an intellectual level, of course, rather than emotional.'

'Right now, all I want is to be at home with my husband and my daughter. Everything else can wait.' Janie paused, looking into the distance. 'You know, if only Olivia had told us the truth about what she saw, about that argument. She must have seen it was Bryony who was arguing with John. If she'd been honest about that, Bryony's crash might have been prevented. Maybe even her own husband's death.'

'I suppose she thought she was protecting Bryony. She didn't want her to be implicated in John's disappearance.'

'Instead she did the opposite, left her unprotected. When she saw them arguing she could have stepped in, confronted John.'

'She'd never have done that. She was probably still in awe of him. They all were. Even you remember?' Janie said.

'Pretty stupid, I know,' Libby said. 'But in my defence I was genuinely interested in hearing about his mum's involvement in the Peace Caravan.'

'I met John's mum a few times,' Will said. 'She never struck me as a campaigner.'

'More Olivia than Clem?' Janie said, winking.

'Yep. It looks like John's plan right from the start of the weekend was to create a false image of himself, making out he was genuinely interested in equality for women. Instead it was all part of a plan to catch Helena and Roger at it, so to speak.' Will's voice faded. Then he extended his hand towards Janie. 'I'm off now, but it's been really good meeting you both and in different circumstances, I'd say it's been a pleasure...'

'Likewise, and good luck with everything, Will.'

They watched him mount his bike and cycle off.

'If we're going to call in at the hospital, we should be going,' Libby said, hesitation in her voice.

Janie didn't need to question the expression on her friend's face, it was evidently one of panic and fear.

'It's okay, Libby, I'll drive us home.'

'What am I going to do, Janie? I have to drive for work. But the thought of sitting behind the wheel still terrifies me.'

'Don't think about it right now. Take a few more days off. While the cuts heal, your nerves will too, you'll see. Once you're at home with your gran everything will fall into place. We might not have been here long, but we've learned enough in this short time to see what needs to be done. You have the perfect opportunity to use your position as a female reporter to champion women's rights, shake up the establishment. Just think of the difference you could make. '

'Now you make me sound like Clem.'

'Nothing wrong with being fired up, passionate for change. You owe it to those who aren't brave enough to stand up and be counted. Think about women like Bryony, forced to hand over her child, just because she isn't married, and Helena, trapped in a marriage with someone who thinks love is about control. You've got a voice, Libby. Use it. And if it means getting behind the wheel of a car now and then, it's a small price to pay, isn't it?'

'One thing's for certain. If my boss gets wind of where I've been this weekend and realises I had the chance of a first-hand scoop, a murder no less, he'll be furious.'

'The local press will have it splashed all over the front page by Monday, I guess.'

'You're right though. I don't want to be that kind of reporter anymore. It's not enough for me just to present the facts, unless those facts are about exposing injustice, questioning the way things are.'

'Will you stay at The Observer?'

'It gives me a voice. What I really need, though, is a weekly column, an editorial slot where I can highlight the issues that affect us all. I'll have to use my powers of persuasion, maybe I'll point out how The Observer could be recognised as a paper that takes a stand on social issues. The thing is there's inequality everywhere you look. Families who work all the hours, but still don't have enough money to pay the bills, and others who are so wealthy they could never spend it all in two lifetimes.'

'I guess there'll always be inequality. We can't hope to eradicate it all.'

'I can make it my mission to try though, can't I? And you're right, if it means getting behind the wheel of my old Mini now and then, it's a very small price to pay.'

'That sounds more like the Libby Frobisher I've come to know and love. Right, I'll just pop through and say goodbye to Peter before we go, then I'll be right with you.'

While Libby returned to their room to pack her case, Janie went through to the kitchen where she found Peter wiping down surfaces.

'I didn't want to leave without saying, goodbye.'

'The police have solved the case, have they? They found the man?'

As Janie ran through recent events, they sounded so matter of fact, as though she was reading one of her much-loved Poirot stories aloud. And yet, these were events that had changed the lives of those involved forever.

'So the man you were looking for wasn't a victim after all?'

'Sadly, he was the perpetrator,' Janie said.

'And they know for sure he's killed someone? I can't imagine how angry you'd have to be to take a man's life.' Peter looked thoughtful. 'I mean I feel angry sometimes, but I could never hurt someone, no matter what they'd done.'

'In truth, none of us know what we would do in the heat of the moment,' Janie said, thinking back to some of the truths she had discovered over the last year. 'When we're faced with a situation where we have to let go of the only thing that drives us on, it can easily tip someone over the edge. I'm guessing John Bramber lost his grip of reality. He'd made himself believe that if he removed each of the obstacles to what he perceived as his perfect marriage, then all would be well. But enough of that, Peter. What about you? Have you decided what you'll do next?'

'Get another job, I guess.'

'And college? You could do both, you know. There are some great evening classes that would help you get into the catering trade. Better still, find an employer that will send you on day release. That way, you'll learn the ropes and have a ready-made job at the end of it.'

'And my parents? Should I try to find them?'

'Only you can answer that one.'

'If I decide to try, will you help me?'

Janie had been away from her everyday life for just three days. In that time she had become embroiled in unravelling potential motives, looking for evidence, challenging people's accounts. Both Bryony and Peter were looking for answers; Bryony desperate to know what happened to her child, Peter longing to know the truth about his parents. Could she help either one, or both?

'Here's my address. There's a good FE college near to where we live. It's your decision, but if you decide to come to Tamarisk Bay be sure to look me up.'

The hospital visit was necessarily short. Bryony was still struggling to stay awake for more than a few minutes, but her firm grip of Libby's hand was an encouraging sign. She was a fighter. Libby had written a short letter, which she slipped into the drawer beside Bryony's bed.

'It's from both of us. Janie and me. You've got our addresses there and we'll be waiting to hear from you as soon as you're well enough.'

There was a lot more Libby wanted to say, but she was struggling to find the right words. John had made Bryony a victim. Not only by causing her car crash, but years ago, when she was a young girl, desperate to belong, to be liked. He made her believe she was worthless. Libby was there when Bryony came close to losing her life. Janie was right. If Libby had come to the weekend conference looking for a purpose, now she had one. She would make it her goal to ferret out the kind of injustices that had brought Bryony to such a dark place and expose them to the light.

It was nearly eight 'o'clock in the evening when Janie walked into her home.

'Greg.' She called her husband's name just once, waiting in the hallway, listening.

Then he was there, coming down the stairs, Michelle in his arms. The sweet scent of talcum powder pervaded the air and before Greg could say a word, Janie embraced them both.

'Oh, it's so good to be home,' she said, her voice muffled against her daughter's blanket.

'She's just had her bath.'

'Dad told you I was coming home?'

'I picked Michelle up at lunchtime. I don't like being in the house when she's not here.'

'I've missed you.' Janie nestled her face in towards her daughter. 'And you,' she said, kissing her husband.

'Michelle isn't the only person who leaves a big empty space; there's a Janie-sized hole in my life when you're not here. And it's only been three days.' Greg lifted Janie's chin a little so that he could look directly at her. 'You know, I've been thinking a lot about us since you left here on Thursday.'

'Me too. It's me who's in the wrong, Greg. I realise that now.'

'I think you forget we're on the same side. I want what you want, whatever will make you happy. You must know how proud I am of you with all you've achieved over the last year. I reckon the main problem is your own self-doubts, you're not too sure what you want. But I really believe you can be anything you want to be, and whatever you choose, I'll support you all the way.'

They moved into the sitting room and sat close together on the sofa, with Michelle nestled between them.

Janie took Greg's hand in hers as she explained. 'It's been a difficult three days in some ways, but strangely it's helped to clarify things too. The conference was all about equality and yet all around me there was inequality. Of the six people in our debating group there was envy, prejudice and misunderstanding on every level. It made me realise that you and I have something special. We're equal partners, we love each and just as importantly we respect each other. I've taken that for granted recently and I want to say sorry.'

'You never need to apologise to me. You know that Love is... cartoon that's cropping up everywhere? Well, I saw one the other day that summed us up. Love is... never having to say you're sorry. So we should make a pact.'

She clasped his hand a bit tighter. 'You know I've been looking forward to this, the three of us snuggling up together, ever since I left here on Thursday. The three of us in harmony. You're right though. It's my own self-doubt that's the real problem. But I've come home full of ideas about what I could do, what I'd like to do. Maybe study?'

'Like I said, whatever you choose I'll support you all the way. And remember, on our own we do okay, but together we're so much more. Like the best bit of brickwork, solid and strong.'

'Brickwork? That's a new one on me.'

'And this little one is the mortar, cementing us together.'

They both gazed down at Michelle, who was happily sucking on her blanket, oblivious to it all.

AUTHOR'S NOTE

DURING MY RESEARCH FOR *A Notable Omission* I gained some fascinating insights into life in England in early 1970.

The Women's Liberation Movement emerged in the late 1960s and held their first conference over several days in late February and early March 1970 at Ruskin College, Oxford University. Some six hundred delegates attended, including some men, who, it is reported, were committed to the movement, hoping for greater social equality for their daughters. In the original conference the recording equipment had to be borrowed. There was no heating and delegates sat in their coats. Nevertheless, the conference was hailed as a great success and the movement went on to organise several more events over subsequent years. Sussex University did not hold one of the conferences, so that element of the novel is purely fictional.

However, the University of Sussex had become known for student radicalism. In March 1970 two hundred students occupied the administration building over fears the university was keeping records of students' political activities. Then, in 1973, a mob of students physically prevented United States government adviser Samuel P. Huntington from giving a speech on campus, because of his involvement in the Vietnam War. Similarly, when the spokesperson for the US embassy, Robert Beers, visited to give a talk to students entitled 'Vietnam in depth' three students were waiting outside Falmer House and threw a bucket of red paint over the diplomat as he was leaving.

Opened in 1961 the University of Sussex was the first university to be established in the UK since the Second World War. (Keele University had also been awarding degrees, but was not granted university status until 1962). The Student Union of the University of Sussex was quite active, organising events and concerts. Performers like Pink Floyd, Jimi Hendrix and Chuck Berry repeatedly performed at the University Common Room, giving the university a reputation for Rock and Roll. It is also true that a team from the University of Sussex won University Challenge in 1967 and 1969.

Although great strides towards greater equality for women had been made over preceding decades there was still much that needed to change. The 1960s in particular saw a young generation discovering their voice, but there was still a bias towards women being employed in the retail sector, or as a cleaner, nurse or secretary, rather than having the opportunity to move into careers that gave them more financial security. And despite women entering higher education in greater numbers, when women were able to break through the career bias they were always paid less than men for the same jobs. The strike by the Dagenham women machinists, referred to in A Notable Omission did take place and helped to set the background for the 1970 Equal Pay Act.

Other events taking place during 1970 include the first award being given to thalidomide victims, the continuing devastation of the Vietnam war, and Concorde making its first supersonic flight. This was also the year before sterling was decimalised, Decimal Day being 15 February 1971, when Britain said goodbye to pounds, shillings and pence.

More than fifty years on from the events chronicled in this story some would argue that much has changed for the better, and others would say that some things have changed for the worse. Whatever your perspective, I hope you have enjoyed this journey back in time.

I take responsibility for any errors, inclusions, or exclusions in the narrative, while reminding readers that this is a work of fiction and any similarities to individuals are purely coincidental.

It's wonderful to receive feedback from readers. It would be lovely to hear your own anecdotes about that period of our history, either from personal memories, or the memories of friends and family.

Comments can be left on my website: www.isabellamuir.com

THANK YOU

THE BEGINNINGS OF THE idea for this story came from a very interesting conversation with our good friend, Ray. He set me thinking and *A Notable Omission* is the result! So, thanks, Ray.

And huge thanks go to fellow author, Lexi Rees, who kindly read through a draft of the novel, providing me with brilliant feedback and suggestions. This final version of *A Notable Omission* is definitely much improved as a result.

And, as always, my love and thanks go to my husband Al, for his patience and support. In the words of one of my favourite songs, he is 'the wind beneath my wings'.

As a reader your words make all the difference
Honest reviews of my books help other readers find them. As an independent author I don't have the backing of a publisher or a team of publicists. I can't advertise in the traditional way, but I do have one thing going for me, and that's a group of engaged readers. If you enjoyed this book I would be very grateful if you could spend just five minutes leaving a review (as short as you like) on Goodreads or your favourite online book review websites, book groups, your own blogs and social media sites.
Thank you!

www.isabellamuir.com